The

Starlight

Barking

also by Dodie Smith:

The Hundred and One Dalmatians

I Capture the Castle

The
Starlight
Barking

Dodie Smith
author of
The Hundred and One Dalmatians

illustrated by
Janet and Anne Grahame-Johnstone

SCHOLASTIC INC.
New York Toronto London Auckland Sydney
Mexico City New Delhi Hong Kong

ISBN 0-439-28594-1

12 11 10 9 8 7 6 5 4 3 2   1 2 3 4 5 6/0

Printed in the U.S.A.   40

First Scholastic printing, March 2001

Contents

The Great Swoosh

The
Starlight
Barking

1. The Mysterious Sleeping

ot long ago there lived in Suffolk a hundred and one Dalmatians whose adventures had once thrilled all the dogs of England. This was when a wicked woman, Cruella de Vil, started a Dalmatian Fur Farm. She imprisoned ninety-seven puppies in a lonely country house named Hell Hall and planned to have their skins turned into fur coats.

Fifteen of the puppies belonged to Pongo and Missis, a young married couple of Dalmatians, who lived in London with a young married couple of humans, Mr. and Mrs. Dearly.

Pongo and Missis rescued *all* the puppies and brought them home to the Dearlys who eventually took them back to that same Hell Hall where they had been imprisoned—it was for sale cheap as Cruella de Vil had fled from England. Hell Hall then became such a happy home that there was talk of changing its name to Heaven Hall. But the Dearlys thought it was just a bit too noisy for heaven.

Of course there were problems to face, the main one being that the hundred and one Dalmatians did not remain only a hundred and one for long. Many of the pups married early and had delightful families. And Mr. Dearly (who was extremely good at arithmetic) foresaw a time when he and Mrs. Dearly would belong to a thousand and one Dalmatians—and more. Large as Hell Hall and its grounds were, they weren't large enough for that, but the Dearlys could not bear the thought of sending so much as one pup away.

And then a splendid thing happened. Some of the dogs made it clear that they actually wanted to go out into the world. They were always trying to climb the high walls or squeeze through the bars of the tall gates. And they showed great affection for visiting tradesmen. The Dearlys realized that these dogs not only wished for adventure; they wished for their own special humans. (Try as they might, the Dearlys could not be the special humans of so very many Dalmatians.) So Mr. Dearly advertised that a few dogs might consider adopting humans, if exactly the right humans could be found.

Naturally he received dozens of replies—the Dalmatians had become so famous at the time of the Great Dog Robbery. So he opened a hostel, in the near-by village, where applicants could stay until they were fully trained and, eventually, chosen by a dog. Dozens of Dearly Dalmatians were now happily settled all over England and the supply never equaled the demand, as the Dearlys liked to keep at least a hundred and one Dalmatians at Hell Hall. Of course nothing would have tempted Pongo and Missis to leave home. And of their fifteen puppies only one had gone out into the world. She was now the best known of all the Dalmatians. More will be told about her soon.

Also settled with the Dearlys for life were the liverspotted Dalmatians, Prince and Perdita, and two white Persian cats. One of these cats had rescued herself from Cruella de Vil and, since then, been married. She and her husband frequently had charming kittens who all went to excellent homes. The household also included Nanny Cook and Nanny Butler who looked after everyone. And now we can start the new story.

One brilliant morning in high summer Pongo woke up with the guilty feeling that he had overslept. But if he had, everyone else in the large, airy bedroom had overslept too. Close behind him his dear wife, Missis, was asleep in her basket, one elegant, black-spotted paw twitching as she raced through a dream. Across the room Prince and Perdita were asleep in their baskets. The white cats were asleep in theirs. Mr. and Mrs. Dearly were asleep in their twin beds. And not one bark, yap or whimper came from below, where the old stables had been made into comfortable kennels. If it had been as late as it felt, an uproar would have broken out by now.

Pongo relaxed, stretched and, as he had no wish to sleep any more, decided to count his blessings. The idea came to him because of something he had thought about the night before. He and all the other dogs had gone for a late walk with the Dearlys and then, after the dogs who slept in the kennels and in the kitchen had been put to bed, each with a good-night biscuit, Pongo, Missis, Prince and Perdita had taken the Dearlys for a last stroll under the stars. Pongo had been delighted to hear that one of these was called the Dog Star.

"It's always particularly bright at this time of the year," said Mr. Dearly. "In fact, these are called the Dog Days."

"Because of the star?" asked Mrs. Dearly.

"I suppose so. All I know is that the Ancient Romans believed that the Dog Star, Sirius, rising with the sun—though one can't see the star in the daylight—adds to the sun's heat and makes the weather specially warm."

"Well, it certainly is, this year," said Mrs. Dearly. "And the star's wonderfully bright."

Pongo then remembered another wonderfully bright star, which had guided him when the weather was very far from warm. He thought of that cold, cold Christmas Eve when he and Missis had rescued all the puppies and were leading them back to London. How terrible it had been when they were pursued by Cruella de Vil in her huge black and white car! But everything had come right and since then there had never been any kind of danger to face. Pongo, strolling, under the stars, told himself he must count his blessings oftener. So now, lying awake in the bright morning, he counted them.

He could always be certain of food, warmth, safety and—most important of all—love (not that a hungry dog can live on love alone). Surely he had everything he wanted? Why, then, was he sometimes just a little bit discontented? What about? It wasn't as if life at Hell Hall was dull; the dogs had plenty of amusements. There were see-saws, swings, a charming little merry-go-round, a small water-shoot into the pond. And often they all went for outings, in two hired motor buses. All the same, whenever he saw a young, adventurous dog proudly leading his newly trained pet out of the tall gates of Hell Hall, while all the resident dogs lined up and barked their good wishes, did he not feel, well, a fraction wistful? He did. And, remembering this now, he found he still felt wistful, and more than a fraction.

Good gracious! What a thing to feel bang in the middle of his blessing counting! And it simply wasn't true. Not for anything in the world would he have left the dear Dearlys. He was *not* wistful. He was a hundred percent happy dog looking forward to another hundred percent happy day—and why didn't the day start? Wasn't anyone but himself going to wake up?

At that moment he heard the stable clock strike the quarter. The Dearlys always got up at seven-thirty so Pongo reckoned it would now be a quarter past seven. But it couldn't, it couldn't be as early as that, not with the sun so high—he could see it through one of the wide open windows. The night had been so warm that the Dearlys had drawn all the curtains back.

He sprang up, ran to a window, and looked at the clock. Then, scarcely believing his eyes, he hurriedly awoke Missis, with a kiss that was really more of a bump on the nose. She instantly said, "Oh dear, have I overslept?"

"Yes, you have and so has everyone else," said Pongo. "Will you kindly tell me what time you make it by the stable clock?"

"Oh, *yes*," said Missis, enthusiastically. She was very proud of being able to tell the time and wished dogs who couldn't would ask her to do so oftener. The reason why they didn't was that she could never remember which hand stood for the hours and which for the minutes. Now, after a long, careful stare, she said, "It's either a quarter past ten or ten to three."

5

"It's a quarter past ten," said Pongo, "and goodness knows that's late enough. Why haven't Mr. and Mrs. Dearly awakened?"

Missis looked anxiously at the Dearlys. "Do you think they're ill?"

"They look particularly well."

"And they're breathing beautifully," said Missis. "In, out, in, out, regular breathing. And Mrs. Dearly's smiling."

"And Mr. Dearly looks as if he might smile at any minute. Yes! He's smiling now."

"They must be having lovely dreams," said Missis. "It seems a shame to wake them. But I think we should."

Just then Prince and Perdita woke up and quickly got the hang of the situation. They, too, thought the Dearlys should be wakened.

"Though they never really like it if we disturb them," said Prince, who was a most considerate dog.

"But this morning it is *necessary*," said Missis, firmly. "Because there are two nursing mothers in the kennels who need good drinks of milk."

"Yes, indeed," said Perdita. "And I promised to help them wash their puppies." Perdita had always been a great puppy-washer.

"Besides, there are young dogs who need their first meal of the day," said Pongo. "I can't think why they're not yapping. Oh, we must certainly disturb the Dearlys. But we'll do it kindly."

Pongo and Prince went to Mr. Dearly. Missis and Perdita went to Mrs. Dearly. All four dogs gave some little *whispered* barks and did some gentle shoulder-patting.

Nothing happened.

The dogs then barked a little louder and patted a little harder. Still nothing happened.

The dogs then barked much louder and patted much harder. But still nothing happened.

"We'd better lick their faces," said Pongo. He knew that the Dearlys, much as they loved their dogs, were not fully appreciative of face-licking, and such an attention was likely to make them sit up briskly. But not today. They just went on sleeping—and also, Pongo was pleased to see, smiling. As he couldn't wake them he was glad not to have spoilt their happy dreams.

Just then Missis accidentally kicked the cats' basket and moved away hastily. Delightful creatures though the cats were, they were always *ready* to be defensive—and who can blame them, when they lived with so very many dogs? Missis, expecting them to spring up, got ready to apologise. But the cats did not stir.

"How very strange," said Missis. And then, greatly daring, she gave both of them a little prod with her paw. The cats, very slightly, flexed their claws; but they did not wake up.

"Perhaps Nanny Cook and Nanny Butler are awake." said Perdita. "Shall Prince and I go and see?"

"Yes, if you can get out of the room," said Pongo. He was clever at lifting latches and drawing back bolts, but the bedroom door had an ordinary handle, and not even the cleverest dog can turn a door handle. He was afraid they were shut up in the room until some human let them out. But as he looked toward the door, it swung open—he could only think that the Dearlys had not quite closed it the night before. Prince and Perdita ran out."

Pongo and Missis made another effort to wake the Dearlys, even biting their ears—tenderly, but quite, quite noticeably; but the Dearlys did *not* notice. They didn't even stop smiling.

Missis then went to an open window and looked out at the sunny morning. After a moment she said, "Pongo, please come here and listen."

Pongo joined her and listened but couldn't hear anything. He told her so.

Missis said, "I meant, listen to the silence. I've never heard it so loud."

"I don't think you can have a loud silence," said Pongo, "but I know what you mean." He listened again, then said, "Missis! There are no birds singing."

"So there aren't," said Missis. "You know, I hardly ever

notice them when they *are* singing, but now—! It's queer that an un-noise can make so much more noise than a noise."

Then Prince and Perdita came back and said they hadn't been able to wake the Nannies.

"Though we tried really hard," said Perdita. "We sat on them and bounced."

"Well, what do we do now?" said Prince, looking eagerly at Pongo. Prince was a brave, intelligent dog but he had never had any adventures such as Pongo had once had, and he was fully prepared to accept Pongo as a leader.

Pongo suddenly felt doubtful of himself. It was so long since he had needed to make important decisions. Was he still capable of doing so? For a moment he felt, well, *almost* stupid— he who was known to own one of the keenest brains in Dogdom!

He shook himself—and then felt dazed as well as stupid. But he was determined not to give himself away. He said, trying to sound confident. "We must find out how far this mysterious sleeping stretches. Missis and I will run to the farm." The truth was that he wanted to consult his good friend, the Old English Sheepdog, the wisest dog he knew.

"Couldn't we save time by just barking to the farm?" said Missis.

"No," said Pongo. "For if we bark loudly we shall wake every dog in Hell Hall and they will all want their breakfasts."

Some people believe that dogs need only one meal a day, and they can manage with this provided the meal is a large one. But the Dearlys thought two meals a day made a dog's life more interesting, and all the Dalmatians were offered a good, light breakfast, and a good, weighty dinner in the late afternoon. Puppies, of course, needed as many as five little meals a day, and Missis now became very anxious about this. She suggested they should be wakened and fed, the small ones by their mothers and the larger ones on bread and milk.

"But we can't get at the milk," said Pongo. "I can't open the refrigerator door. Later, Prince and I can lift the lids of the biscuit bins, so all the grown-up dogs can have something. But we shall need help with the puppies and nursing mothers."

"Then we'd better set about getting it," said Missis.

Pongo gave Prince instructions. "If any dogs wake up, you and Perdita must explain and keep them as calm as possible. Say we shall soon be back. In case of any emergency, just bark for advice. Take good care of Mr. and Mrs. Dearly. I have complete confidence in you."

Prince looked, and felt, extremely proud. He—the hundred and oneth Dalmatian—had so often wished he had been a member of the household in those dangerous days when the missing puppies had to be found and rescued. And he was always anxious to show how grateful he was to Pongo and Missis for sharing the Dearlys with him and Perdita. "Count on me," he said sturdily.

"And of course we count on Perdita, too," said Missis, kindly. She sometimes thought Perdita's mania for washing puppies—and people—a bit silly, but was very fond of her.

"Then off we go," said Pongo.

As he and Missis ran downstairs, he wondered how they would get out of the house. It was a long time since he had opened a window and he hoped he still had the knack of it. But as they reached the hall he saw that the front door was a little bit open.

"What wonderful luck," he said, as he and Missis ran out

into the garden. He now planned to get out by way of the old stone Folly—the Sheepdog had shown him how to do this, in the days when Hell Hall was the enemy's camp. But as he looked across the pond at the front of the house he saw that the tall iron gates were not quite closed. What *had* the Dearlys been thinking of last night? As a rule, these gates were not only closed but also locked.

Now they were only just open and Missis was afraid they might be too heavy to be pushed open wide enough. But as the dogs approached the gates swung inwards.

"How nice of the wind to help us," said Missis, as they ran through the gates—which instantly closed behind them. "Oh, how peculiar! The wind must be blowing both ways."

"But there *isn't* any wind," said Pongo.

2. News from Downing Street

It was true. There wasn't a breath of wind. And the stillness, combined with the silence, made the sunny morning feel very strange indeed.

"Of course the stillness makes the silence louder," said Missis, "because as well as there being no birds singing—and no insects buzzing or whirring their wings, I've just noticed—there's no rustling, no leaves or grasses stirring. But somehow I quite like the feel of it, and I like the way *I* feel, most unusually light."

"Perhaps that's because you haven't had any breakfast," said Pongo. "I should have found you some biscuits."

"I couldn't have eaten a mouthful. Oh, that doesn't mean that I'm ill. I'm just unhungry."

"Dear Missis, that's a world's record," said Pongo.

Missis smiled. Her good appetite was a family joke.

"What's more I can't imagine being hungry. And I suddenly know something. When all the dogs at Hell Hall wake up, *they* won't be hungry, either."

"You can't be sure of that just because *you're* not hungry."

"Well, if I can't imagine myself being hungry, I can't imagine their being hungry, can I? Anyway, they won't be. Are *you* hungry, Pongo?"

"Well, no. But that may be because I'm anxious."

"I'm not. I'm puzzled, of course, but that's interesting. And I suppose I'm excited. *I* know how I feel. Do you remember when you persuaded me to try the watershoot? There I was, at the top of the shoot, looking down at the pond. I wasn't exactly frightened, because you were there and the Dearlys were standing by and, anyway, I can swim. But I did feel, well, just as I feel now and it's really quite pleasant. And talking of swimming, how easy it is to run this morning, more like swimming through air."

"Now that you mention it—" Pongo realized that he was, indeed, moving with great ease but he had too much on his mind to enjoy it. For as well as being anxious about the mysterious sleeping, he was so afraid he might not be equal to— well, whatever he had to be equal to.

Just then, Missis saw two horses asleep in a field and said cheerfully, "Breathing nicely, aren't they?" Then she suddenly stopped running. "Oh, Pongo look!"

Curled up in a grassy nest was a sleeping mouse.

Pongo said hastily, "Missis, dear, I wouldn't." For Missis was a famous mouse-chaser.

She looked at him haughtily. "I wouldn't dream of pouncing on the poor little creature. It's only when they run that they're so tempting. Mice shouldn't imitate toys."

The farm was now in sight and, as Pongo and Missis drew near to it, they at last saw someone who wasn't asleep. The Old English Sheepdog came running to meet them, at a surprising speed for such a large, elderly dog (large even under his enormously thick, woolly coat) who was often a little short of breath.

In the days when he had helped to rescue the Dalmatian puppies he had been a Colonel. Afterwards, with every justification, he had made himself a General. He had always remained on the friendliest terms with Pongo and Missis and often visited Hell Hall. Now he said, "I was coming to see you. Oh, my dear young friends, I'm afraid the fact that you're here means that you, also, are faced with a dangerous situation."

"Then your humans are unwakeable too?" said Pongo.

"All of them, including my dear young Tommy, who's usually so very wide-awake. But it isn't only the humans who are asleep. Come and see for yourselves."

The General led the way. They saw sleeping ducks around the pond, sleeping hens in their pen, sleeping pigeons in their dovecote up in the gable of the barn. A gentle snoring came from the pig-sty and no sound whatever from the cow-shed. Missis at once went to make sure that all cows were breathing satisfactorily; she had loved them ever since that night when they had given drinks of warm milk to the hungry, rescued puppies.

14

"And I've been to my sheep in the meadow," said the General. "I couldn't make the slightest impression on them. Now come and look at my poor Mrs. Willow."

Pongo and Missis followed him into the kitchen. The tabby cat lay in her basket, utterly asleep.

"Never before has she let me down," said the General.

"As you know, I think of her more as a dog than a cat. I still can't quite believe . . ." He kicked the basket and said in a very military voice, "Wake up, Major!" Then he added tenderly, "Puss, *please!*"

But the tabby cat went on sleeping.

Pongo said, "It's been worse for you than for Missis and me, General. We had Prince and Perdita to talk to. You've had no one." For the Sheepdog was the only dog at the farm.

"Well, I'll admit I was pretty thankful to see you two. Not that I allowed myself to get *too* alarmed, once I saw that all humans and all creatures look perfectly healthy." The General then turned to Missis. "Still, I'd like a female opinion on young Tommy."

They went along to Tommy's room. Though he was still young enough to sleep in his small painted bed, he now thought himself too old to play with the little blue cart he had once lent to help the Dalmatian puppies get back to London. But it was there, on top of the toy cupboard, and Missis gave it a grateful look. Then she assured the Sheepdog that Tommy seemed particularly well. "Beautifully rosy cheeks, and magnificent breathing."

"Such an intelligent boy," said the General, glancing proudly at the books on the bedside table.

"Can he read already?" asked Pongo.

"Well, not the words, but he reads the pictures splendidly.

16

He's particularly fond of something he calls Science Fiction. Don't understand it myself, of course. It seems very mysterious."

"So I've gathered from television," said Pongo. "I'm sure Tommy would be extremely interested in this mysterious sleeping if he wasn't a mysterious sleeper himself. Hello, what's that?"

They all heard a high, shrill barking.

"Bless me, that's Cadpig," said Missis.

"No, Missis," said Pongo. "Her barking couldn't carry all the way from London."

"Well, it's certainly some dog wanting something," said the Sheepdog. "Let's go outside."

They ran out into the farmyard. The shrill barking continued and now they could make out what was being barked. "Calling Pongo, Missis or the General!"

"Good gracious, it *is* Cadpig!" said Pongo, and he answered at the top of his bark, "Hearing you loud and clear! Where are you, my dear?"

"At home of course," barked Cadpig.

"At home? Do you mean you're back at Hell Hall?"

"Certainly not," replied Cadpig, sounding a little bit grand. "*My* home is at Number Ten, Downing Street."

And now we must learn what had been happening to the smallest, prettiest and bossiest of the fifteen puppies born to Pongo and Missis when they, like the Dearlys, had been "young marrieds." A year or so before this story begins, Mr. Dearly—not for the first time—had been asked by the Government to help it get out of debt. He had driven to London and with him, under the seat, went Cadpig, who had heard him say where he was going. When he got out of the car at

No. 10 Downing Street, out shot Cadpig so fast that she got through the front door before he did. As the Government was now so worried, the Prime Minister was waiting in the hall to receive Mr. Dearly. Cadpig, who had seen the P.M. on television, recognized him instantly, flung herself at him, and treated him with such slavish affection that he was extremely flattered. A policeman who attempted to remove Cadpig was waved aside and she was allowed (looking both smug and winsome) to attend the financial discussion.

The Government had now got itself into such trouble that even Mr. Dearly didn't know how to get it out. He had at one time been called a wizard of finance but he now felt that a real wizard of magic (plus some kindly gnomes) was needed. Still, he did his best and also said he must put his thinking cap on. (Cadpig thought this an insincere remark, as she knew he didn't own any kind of hat.) He then got up to go and called Cadpig to follow him. She had been lying at the Prime Minister's feet. Now she sprang up, pushed the P.M. back into his armchair, jumped onto his knee and hid her head inside his jacket.

Mr. Dearly apologized for her and said—quite sternly—"Come on, Cadpig!" She then tried to burrow into the Prime Minister's chest. Mr. Dearly took hold of her collar—and she then flung her paws around the Prime Minister's neck, kissing him and whimpering between kisses. Mr. Dearly, who knew that Cadpig was not a sentimental dog, was astonished at this quite mawkish behaviour. But the Prime Minister was now much more than flattered. He was deeply touched. Tears sprang to his eyes—nowadays he was so often criticized, and even bullied, so seldom treated kindly. He begged to be allowed to keep Cadpig. And Mr. Dearly, seeing that nothing but brute force would dislodge her, felt he must agree.

Not long after this, the Prime Minister spoke on television. Cadpig had loved television since she was a tiny puppy and longed to appear on it. Indeed, that was her main reason for coming to Downing Street. She had a little plan. Just before the Prime Minister finished his speech she came out from behind a curtain, climbed up him, and showed him so much love that his popularity was enormously increased—the British Nation said "Dogs always *know*." Since then she had been with him for all his television speeches and she had taken to wrinkling her nose at the Nation in a very fetching smile. She only did this at the end of his speech, so no one ever turned him off half way through. She also eased the tension when very cross people came to see him; and, one way and another, she was a terrific success. Most members of the Government hastily bought dogs, but none of these were as important as she was.

And now it was this brilliant daughter who was calling her parents and the General. And it was her own bark they were hearing. Pongo was amazed. As a rule, conversation to London—over sixty miles away—had to be relayed by nearly five hundred dogs. (How well Pongo remembered this, from the time when the Twilight Barking chain had brought news of his stolen puppies!) He said, "How on earth are you managing it, Cadpig? Is it some new invention?"

"Never mind that now," said Cadpig. "Just tell me if things are the same with you as they are here. Everyone asleep but dogs?"

"Every living creature," said Pongo.

"It's happened all over England—I've had dozens of reports.

And I think it may be world-wide—not that I've been able to get in touch with dogs out of England yet, but I hope to soon."

"How?" said Pongo. "You can't bark across the sea."

"Not bark, exactly but—well, I'm barking to you and you're barking to me but I'm almost sure we're *really* reaching each other by thought waves—it's all part of the strangeness this morning. And I think I can extend my thought waves, when I've had more practice. But all that matters now is that I want you and Mother to start for London at once."

"My dear child!" said Pongo, much honored. "Of course we'll come. Unless—just a minute, Cadpig." He turned to Missis and began to relay what Cadpig had said.

Missis interrupted him. As a rule she had difficulty in catching everything said on long-distance barking but today she had heard every word. "I'm willing, Pongo," she said eagerly.

"You don't think we ought to keep guard over the Dearlys?"

"Prince and Perdita can do that."

"Of course they can," said Cadpig. She had heard what they said although they had used low tones of bark. "And I *must* have you here. Delegations of dogs are coming from all over England. I need Mother to help me on the social side and you, Father, must advise me politically."

"You know as much about politics as I do," said Pongo.

"Probably much more, by now," said Cadpig, who had never been famous for modesty. "I really meant *strategically*. You were splendid at strategy when you saved us all from Cruella de Vil."

"I was helped by the General," said Pongo, sounding more modest than he felt. He was really puffed up with pride at his famous daughter's praise.

"Well, the General had better come to London, too."

But the General barked loudly, "Sorry, but I can't leave Tommy and Mrs. Willow."

"Oh, bother," said Cadpig. "This is no time for personal loyalties. The fate of Dogdom may be at stake. Still, you can advise me by thought waves, can't you?"

"I doubt it," said the Sheepdog. "I'm much too bewildered."

"Well, who isn't?" said Cadpig. "We've just got to be prepared for *anything*. Now, Father, I reckon it will take you and Mother a little over two hours to reach London."

"Two hours!" gasped Pongo. "It took us over two *days* when we ran here from London to rescue you all. And we were younger then."

"But things are different now," said Cadpig. "Now listen carefully. This morning, when I couldn't wake the Prime Minister, I was in a great hurry to get help. I dashed down the stairs at full speed and wished I could go faster—and then I found I *was* going faster. I was skimming over the stairs without touching them, like flying but my feet were only just off the ground. At first I thought I'd merely done a wonderful jump, but I've discovered that I can do it all the time, and so can all the dogs who've come to ask my advice. We've been practising it up and down Downing Street. It's a sort of *swoosh*; you float on the air and you can regulate your speed just by thinking about it. Do you understand?"

"I understand what you're saying," said Pongo. "But I can't imagine myself—"

"But that's what you *must* do, Father. You must *imagine* yourself swooshing and then you *will* swoosh."

"But I'm a very solid dog. Oh, good gracious!" Pongo broke off, staring in astonishment.

Missis was swooshing around the farmyard.

"I can do it, I can do it!" she cried triumphantly.

And now the Sheepdog was swooshing, too.

"Try it, Father," commanded Cadpig.

Well, if the burly General could swoosh! Pongo launched himself forward—and only managed a jump.

"You're over-anxious," said the General. "Take it calmly."

Pongo took it calmly, but only managed a calm jump.

Missis, swooshing past him gracefully, called, "Remember that Hovercraft we saw on television. Imagine yourself a Hovercraft, Pongo."

Pongo vividly remembered the Hovercraft. He thought of it skimming over the waves, just above the waves. And then . . . He found himself skimming over the land.

It felt delightful, no effort at all. He increased his speed and soon outdistanced Missis and the General.

Missis barked to Cadpig, "Your father's a magnificent swoosher now."

"Nothing to it, really," said Pongo. "What do you reckon our top speed is, Cadpig?"

"The Minister of Transport's dog has been timing us. She thinks we can do about thirty miles an hour. And she says that should be our speed limit. I've agreed—it's best to humor her; she's doing a very good job—but we've really no way of judging our speed limit, so just come as fast as you can."

Pongo, after one last burst of speed, pulled up, saying, "Amazing. I just don't understand it."

"There are plenty of things I don't understand this morning," said Cadpig. "What about the extraordinary behavior of doors? They open when one wants them to, otherwise I should still be shut up in the Prime Minister's bedroom."

So that was it. The Dearlys had *not* left the doors open last night.

Missis, still swooshing, said, "The strangest thing of all is that I'm not hungry."

"No dogs are," said Cadpig. "Which is a blessing, as I couldn't arrange food for all the dogs who are coming to London—though I suppose I could if I needed to, if I really set my *mind* on it. I'm pretty sure this whole business is metaphysical. Don't you agree, Father?"

"Well, yes and no," said Pongo, deciding that before he met Cadpig he somehow had to find out what "metaphysical" meant.

"Now I must go," said Cadpig. "I've dozens of things to do. Oh, I almost forgot. Please bring a strong force of Dalmatians with you. I may form a private army—which you will command, Father—and we shall need plenty of our own breed."

Missis stopped swooshing. "Why do we have to have an army? Must we fight someone?"

"I hope not, Mother. But we must be prepared."

"But if everyone but us is asleep, who is there to fight?"

"I don't know, Mother. And the enemy you don't know is worse than the enemy you know."

"Nonsense," said Missis. "The enemy you don't know isn't there."

"Anyway, please get to me quickly."

Pongo and Missis promised they would. Then the barking ended and the sunny morning was silent and still again.

Pongo said, "How strange that we actually heard her voice across more than sixty miles!"

"No stranger than hearing voices on the telephone," said Missis.

"But a telephone has wires. Cadpig's thoughts were traveling direct from her mind to ours."

"Well, no stranger than television, anyway. *That* doesn't have wires."

"But there are lots of complicated things inside a television set," said Pongo.

"And there are lots of complicated things inside our minds," said Missis.

The General then urged them to hurry back to Hell Hall and collect their army. "And mind you choose good soldiers," he told them.

Missis said, "None of them are *any* kind of soldiers They're just dogs. And do let's go on thinking of them as dogs—for as long as we can."

3. The Meaning of Metaphysical

ow that they could swoosh, Pongo and Missis got back to Hell Hall in a couple of minutes. Remembering how light they had felt, when running to the farm, Pongo guessed they had almost swooshed by instinct and he was annoyed with himself for needing to be taught by Cadpig. He must be more alert. And he must certainly find Mr. Dearly's dictionary and learn what "metaphysical" meant.

Missis was happy to discover that she could swoosh sitting, as well as on four legs. It would make a restful change on the long journey to London. She then became worried because they wouldn't have their collars on as they couldn't put them on for themselves. "Suppose we meet a policeman?"

"All the policemen will be asleep," Pongo reminded her.

"Well, that's something to be thankful for."

As the gates of Hell Hall swung open to let them in they saw that the front lawn was packed with Dalmatians.

Prince hurried forward to say, "They all woke up soon after you left. I explained, and there was no panic whatsoever. None of them are hungry but they seem perfectly well, and more peaceful than usual."

"So I see," said Pongo, astonished.

At this time of the morning the Dearly Dalmatians were usually at their most boisterous and there was keen competition for the water-shoot, see-saw and swings. Today only the younger dogs were playing. The elder dogs sat still, looking expectant but calm.

Pongo congratulated Prince on the way he had handled things.

"Perdita helped, of course," said Prince. "The nursing mothers were a little worried because their puppies had no appetite. But Perdita soothed them. And every pup will start the Emergency spotlessly clean."

Under a shady tree, Perdita could be seen puppy-washing.

"Naturally, everyone's eager for news," Prince went on, "but I've asked them not to rush you."

Pongo, gazing at the sunny, dog-filled lawn, disliked disturbing so much peace, but it had to be done. He stepped forward between Missis and Prince, called all dogs to attention and told them what he had learned from Cadpig. When he described swooshing there was a ripple of movement—many dogs wanted to try it. But Pongo restrained them.

"A swooshing class will be held later," he said firmly. "*Now* we have to decide who's coming to London. Mothers with puppies must, of course, stay here, and fathers of puppies must stay and guard their families. All other dogs are free to volunteer. I'd like a show of tails."

Instantly the whole lawn seethed with wildly wagging tails.

"Thank you, thank you," said Pongo. "But I mustn't take so many." He turned to Prince. "I think we'd better discuss it, while Missis holds a swooshing class—in the yew walk, I suggest. That's long enough for them to practice speed."

The yew walk was a stretch of grass between two tall yew hedges. Missis, feeling important, led the way there. Every dog except Pongo and Prince went with her. Even the nursing mothers took their puppies to watch.

Pongo then asked Prince if he would stay and guard the Dearlys. "I shan't feel at ease unless you do. And of course Perdita must stay with you and as many dogs as you think are needed here."

Prince would have liked to go to London, but he knew where his duty lay as he and Perdita were half-owners of the Dearlys. He also knew that Perdita was a home-loving dog—having been, during a tragic period of her youth, homeless. So he agreed to stay and said Pongo must take all the dogs he wished. "All my own family will want to come," said Pongo. "What a blessing that Lucky's chosen a wife as bright as he is. They'll be a great help. So will Patch. And he's longing to see Cadpig."

Patch had never married. He had found out that, for the

good of the Dalmatian breed, he ought not to hand on his patched ear. But he had not been unhappy. He had become a sort of uncle dog and was tremendously popular with puppies. He was always ready to play with them and he loved them all. But the great love of his life was his sister, Cadpig, of whom he had taken such care when she was a tiny, weak puppy. He was proud of her fame, but he had never ceased to miss her.

Pongo went on, "I wonder if I can risk taking Roly Poly."

The fat pup who had had so many accidents was now a fat dog who still had accidents—and as he was larger, *they* were larger. At that very moment there was a roar of laughter from the dogs in the yew walk and Missis was heard saying, "Oh dear, have you hurt yourself, Roly? You're not supposed to swoosh *through* things."

"We'd better see what's happening," said Pongo.

They found that Roly Poly hadn't done himself any harm, though he hadn't done a yew hedge any good. Pongo whispered to Missis, "I hardly feel it will be safe to take Roly with us."

"Neither will it be safe to leave him behind," said Missis. "And I'd rather know the worst about him than just imagine the worst."

"And his feelings would be terribly hurt if we didn't take him. I'm afraid some dogs are bound to have their feelings hurt."

But things didn't turn out that way. It was taken for granted that Pongo would want his own family. And when he and Prince divided the remainder up, like choosing sides in a game (no married couples were separated), the ones who were to remain behind at once took to the idea of guarding the Dearlys and defending Hell Hall, though no one knew what from. It was all part of the perfect behavior of all dogs on that remarkable morning.

None of the dogs had any difficulty in learning to swoosh, but Pongo wanted to be sure that all the dogs coming to London were strong swooshers, so he left them to practice while he and Missis took a last look at their pets.

First they ran up to the big, comfortable attic which was shared by the Nannies. Nanny Cook, in a frilly nightgown, slept with her mouth open. Nanny Butler, in pyjamas, slept with her mouth firmly shut. They both looked comfortable and spendidly healthy.

"How kind they've always been to us," said Missis. "Do you remember that night when they helped to wash the soot off us and all the puppies?"

Pongo said, "That was when we were at the end of an adventure. Now we're at the beginning of one."

"Well, thank goodness this one can't have anything to do with Cruella de Vil," said Missis, "as we know she had to leave England."

"But—" Pongo broke off in time. Some months earlier he had heard the Dearlys saying that Cruella had come back. He had kept this from Missis at the time and he would go on keeping it from her. And, anyway, how could Cruella have anything to do with this mysterious sleeping?

They ran down to the Dearlys' bedroom. Nothing had changed. The Dearlys still smiled in their sleep. The white cats, if not actually smiling, were looking as blissful as sleeping cats can.

Missis gave her basket a loving look, then suddenly cried, "Pongo, I've just remembered! Last night I had an important dream." As a rule, Missis dreamt about food. In good dreams, jam-tarts grew on trees and chocolate drops came down like rain, and so on. In bad dreams food was often behind glass or in tins that couldn't be opened. But this last dream was different from any dream she had ever had before and she wasn't sure if it was good or bad. She only knew it was important. "There was a dazzling bright light," she told Pongo. "And—oh dear, I can't remember any more."

"Perhaps it will come back to you," said Pongo, though he rather hoped it wouldn't. He enjoyed telling his own dreams, but wasn't fond of listening to other people's. "I think we should start now, my dear."

So they kissed the Dearlys and looked very kindly at the cats. And Missis told her basket she would soon be home (she did this silently because Pongo would have laughed at her for talking to her basket). And then they ran downstairs.

When they reached the hall Pongo said, "Let's go into Mr. Dearly's study. I want to find out the meaning of that strange word Cadpig used, 'metaphysical'. It'll be in that dictionary."

Pongo was a splendid reader—how often had he blessed those Alphabet Blocks he had played with as a pup! But he had never looked up a word in the dictionary and he wasn't sure on which shelf the dictionary was kept. Also, the room was only dimly lit because the curtains were still drawn. But as he peered around, a shaft of sunlight came between the curtains (did they draw aside just a little to let it in?) and it shone full on a dark blue book which had "Dictionary" in gold letters on its back. He nosed it from the shelf and it slid gently to the floor, where it fell open. The bright shaft of sunlight shone on it.

"Bless me, it's opened at the very word I want," said Pongo.

"I do call that civil," said Missis.

Pongo found the words which explained "metaphysical" as puzzling as the word itself. But when he read them aloud to Missis she understood two of them, "visionary" and "supernatural." She said "visionary" was when you imagined things, and "supernatural" must mean extra specially natural.

"Or perhaps more than natural," said Pongo. "And I see that metaphysics has something to do with the mind."

Missis said, "*I* think metaphysical means magic—a kind of magic that comes from our own minds. That's why we're able to open doors today, and talk direct to Cadpig—and swoosh. Oh, Pongo, I *like* metaphysical!"

"I don't think I do," said Pongo. "I don't think I like things I don't understand."

"That's because you have such a splendid brain. *My* brain understands so little that it loves things it's not *supposed* to understand. Anyway, I've taken to metaphysical."

Pongo never thought Missis as silly as she thought herself. And he greatly depended on her instincts. He was a clever dog and he knew it. But he also knew that the cleverer he got, the less help he got from his instincts. So he was happy that he could rely on what his dear wife often called her "feelings." And if she was in favor of metaphysical he would do his best to be, too.

He tried to put the dictionary back on its shelf, but could not manage it. Why? When this morning he could do so many things not usually possible?

"It's because you don't *need* to," said Missis. "If you did,

I'm sure metaphysical would help. The book will be quite safe on the floor."

"Not if any puppies get in here."

So Missis pushed the book under the sofa with her nose and said, "No puppy will find it there. And when we come back and Mr. Dearly's awake we'll show him where his dictionary is."

But *would* they ever come back? *Would* Mr. Dearly ever wake? Pongo tried to turn these fears out of his mind. Anyway, he must hide them from Missis. He said briskly, "Now we must hurry."

They ran out into the sunny garden.

4. The Great Swoosh

y now the fifty Dalmatians who were coming to London were accomplished swooshers. Pongo lined them up on the front lawn in rows of four. He and Missis were in the front row with Patch and Roly Poly. Lucky and his wife, Gay, were in the back row to see there were no stragglers. In between, dotted about, were the other members of Pongo's family. They were looking forward to seeing their famous sister, Cadpig, in Downing Street.

When they were ready to start Pongo said to Missis, "It does seem strange to set out without so much as a drink of water. Shall I ask if any dog is thirsty?"

"Ask if you like, but no dog will be—any more than we are."

Still, Pongo asked. But though the pond was at hand (which the dogs found more tasty than tap water) no dog wanted to drink.

"Very peculiar," said Pongo.

"Just metaphysical," said Missis.

Pongo had a few last words with Prince, Missis kissed Perdita affectionately, and all the dogs who were staying behind wished the little army good luck. Then Pongo said, "Now we'll start very slowly. Then take your pace from Missis and me, and be ready to stop at the farm. I must have a word with the General. Gates, please!"

The tall gates swung open, and out at a slow swoosh went the thirteen rows of four Dalmatians. Then the gates swung together again.

When they were out on the road Pongo increased the pace and they reached the farm quickly—to find that a Beagle, two Spaniels, a very brave Pekingese and four dogs of mixed breed were lined up and ready to join up.

The sheepdog said, "I swooshed to the village and recruited them. And I've got myself a bright lad to train as a lieutenant." He glared down at a small Jack Russell Terrier, "Not that he'll ever be as good as Mrs. Willow, or as Lucky was at his age."

"Yes, I will. I'll be better," said the Jack Russell Terrier, in a shrill voice, glaring back at the Sheepdog.

"Bless my soul, what impertinence," said the General. "Still, I like a bit of spirit." One reason that the General was so fond

of the tabby cat was that she always answered him back and there was no doubt that the Jack Russell was going to be just as good at it.

Lucky had now got the eight dogs from the village into line.

"My guess is that you'll be joined by volunteers all along the route," said the General, "which is bound to delay you. So you'd better get a move on."

"All dogs at the ready," said Pongo and then, after saying goodbye to the General and the Jack Russell, he commanded, "Quick swoosh!"

The road from the farm twisted, so the swoosh wasn't really quick at first. But after they were through the village—where all the dogs who were remaining on guard raised a hearty cheer—they were soon on the high road and could go full speed. Pongo found there was no need to bark instructions. Whatever pace he set was instantly followed. He found this puzzling and asked Missis if she could explain it.

Missis at once said, "It's quite simple. You think a faster thought and we all go faster. You think a slower thought and we all slow down. Indeed, we only move forward at all because you think a forward thought."

Just then there was a terrific commotion. Roly Poly swooshed backwards and bumped into the dog behind him, and that dog bumped into the dog that was behind *him*, and so on right to the back row of the army. Pongo both thought and barked "Halt!" and was thankful no one was hurt.

"But whatever happened, Roly?" he asked, while the dogs behind were picking themselves up.

"I was listening to what you and Mother were saying," said Roly Poly. "And I accidentally thought a *backward* thought."

"No one but your Father is to think any thoughts at all," said Missis. "And you'd better warn all the other dogs, Pongo."

But Pongo didn't think this would be wise. "It might make them nervous. And no dog but Roly Poly would think a backward thought when we're swooshing forward. All will be well if Roly will make his mind a blank."

"I'll try. I'll try hard," said Roly Poly.

The swoosh began again but this time Roly didn't budge and was knocked down by the dog behind him. Again the army had to halt. Missis said, "He made his mind *too* blank—it didn't let your thoughts in, Pongo. Roly, dear, tell your mind that it's to do what your father's mind tells it. Just until we get to London. Then you can think your own thoughts again."

After that, they swooshed smoothly until they reached the town of Sudbury. Pongo, looking at the closed shops, thought

of all the pleasant shopkeepers, now fast asleep. He knew many of them well as the Dearlys often brought him and Missis here on market days. How jolly—and noisy—the market had always been! Now it was deserted except for a group of dogs standing by Gainsborough's statue, waiting to join the army. Pongo halted so that Lucky could fit them in.

Missis, looking up at the church clock, said, "Twelve o'clock, my favourite time! Both hands are in the same place so I can't get them mixed." Then, as the clock began to chime, she added, "Oh, Pongo, do you remember? It was striking twelve the first time we saw this town, when we came to rescue the puppies. But then it was striking midnight, which makes quite a different noise."

"Not really," said Pongo.

"Well, it does to me—because the *feel* of midnight is just a little scaring and the feel of midday isn't. Though today even midday feels a bit peculiar."

Soon they were on their way again and swooshing through beautiful open country. It was a marvellous high summer day, in fact Missis thought it was the highest summer day she had ever known. The sky seemed farther away than usual and looked more like blue velvet than a normal sky does; Missis felt she would like to stroke it. Tall trees looked particularly tall and their heavy foliage looked particularly soft and furry. Cornfields were turning gold and the very air seemed golden and not just because the sun was shining; the air seemed to have a golden haze of its own. And the whole countryside was utterly still.

Missis said, "Isn't it strange that, though we're moving so fast, our ears aren't blowing back?"

"And I can't feel any breeze on my nose," said Pongo.

"All the winds, like all the creatures but dogs, must be asleep. Pongo, I *am* enjoying this peaceful swoosh."

Pongo felt it wasn't safe to feel peaceful. But he didn't want to worry Missis so he told her to go on enjoying herself.

"You mean, as long as I can," said Missis, guessing that his sense of responsibility was making him anxious. "And so I will. But I could enjoy myself much more if *you* were enjoying yourself. Do try. Remember that enjoyment's something you can store up. Once you've had it, no one can take it away."

"That's a fine maxim, my dear."

"A what, Pongo?"

"A maxim. It's a word I've heard Mr. Dearly use. I think it means something you specially believe in."

"Fancy me speaking a maxim!" said Missis, proudly. "Anyway, try to relax. Perhaps there may be worries ahead of us, but don't let's meet them half way."

So Pongo relaxed and the whole army of Hover-dogs swooshed peacefully through the still, silent morning, stopping only when dogs were waiting to join the army. But the worries that lay ahead were soon reaching out toward them. While they were waiting for Lucky to fit some dogs in, Pongo felt a sudden stirring in his mind and, a moment later, he heard Cadpig barking. (The thought wave had come just ahead of the bark—like light traveling faster than sound.) He answered at once.

"Thank goodness I've found you," said Cadpig. "It isn't easy to get in touch with dogs who are on the move. Where are you and how soon will you be at No. 10?"

Pongo said he thought they were about half way and would be at least another hour.

"You're being terribly slow," said Cadpig.

Pongo explained that they sometimes had to stop for dogs who wanted to come with them.

Cadpig brushed this aside. "Let them come on their own."

"But they don't know the way," said Pongo. "I do, because I've often driven to London with Mr. Dearly."

"They can get to London if they *think* about getting to London," said Cadpig. "I've had that information barked all over England. But some dogs just want to be led. Anyway, far too many dogs are coming. There's a seething mass of dogs outside No. 10. Oh Father, do hurry!"

"Anything specially wrong, dear?" asked Missis.

"Nothing I can bark about. But I do have a lot on my mind. I must go, I'm being called—I think we may be getting through to America. Now swoosh your fastest, but look out for traffic when you get near London."

"Traffic?" said Pongo, astonished.

"I mean dog traffic, of course. There are dog jams all over the place. Get as close to Downing Street as you can and then bark to me. I'll send an escort. Goodbye for now."

All the dogs had heard Cadpig so Pongo only had to give the order "Full swoosh ahead" and set the fastest pace he could. Missis didn't care for it at all. She said, "All the peace is gone. Well, Cadpig never was a peaceful dog. Pongo, did you think she sounded scared?"

Pongo had, indeed, thought so but he didn't want to worry Missis, so he just said, "Perhaps it was simply that her voice was a little tired. She must have done a powerful lot of barking this morning. Well, we shall soon be there to help her."

There were now fewer waiting dogs who had to be stopped for, as many of them had started on their own. But when, after a long, fast swoosh, the outskirts of London were reached, traffic problems began and it was no longer possible to swoosh fast. Dogs were coming from all directions, in small groups and long processions, it was difficult to judge who had the right of way. Pongo wished the traffic lights were working—and suddenly they were! He didn't feel he was a sufficiently powerful wisher to have done this on his own, so he could only think that Cadpig had somehow arranged it.

As they got closer and closer to the heart of London, the streets looked stranger and stranger. There were no humans anywhere, there was no traffic but dogs, all the shops were closed; but wherever there were houses, some front doors were open and dogs were sitting there watching the passing dogs. Nowhere was there any sign of panic. Indeed, the watching dogs looked particularly calm, expectantly calm.

Missis, while they were waiting at traffic lights, said, "Doesn't it strike you as peculiar that there's so little noise? It isn't normal for dogs to be so silent."

"I think they're listening," said Pongo. "And perhaps they're learning to hear with a sort of inner ear."

"Well, I don't think it's healthy," said Missis. "Sometimes the young dogs at Hell Hall make more noise than I care for, but I'd be glad enough to hear it now. And I don't think I hold with inner ears—or thought waves. How can one be sure one's keeping one's thought to oneself? One's entitled to *private* thoughts."

Pongo was about to say something soothing when he saw a look of horror come into his wife's eyes. He said quickly, "What is it? What's wrong?" Then he saw what she was looking at.

Partly hidden by some small houses was a factory with a

signboard on the top of it on which was painted, in scarlet, CRUELLA DE VILL & CO. Makers of KLOES THAT KLANK.

KLOES THAT KLANK? To Pongo it didn't make sense. But it did to Missis because she was a bad speller. She said at once "It means Clothes that Clank. But all that matters is that she's back in England—that wicked woman!"

Pongo now confessed that he had known. "But she's not our enemy now, Missis. She won't want Dalmatian skins any more. Mr. de Vil's no longer a furrier. The Dearlys said he and Cruella are making plastic raincoats."

"Plastic raincoats don't clank," said Missis. "And clanking clothes sound dangerous. Up till now I've quite enjoyed this adventure but if Cruella's back—"

"She can't have anything to do with what's happening to-day," said Pongo. "Just try to keep your mind off her. See, the traffic lights are changing."

Missis was only too glad to move past the factory but she went on worrying and after a few minutes she said, "We must warn Cadpig. She must have Cruella locked up."

"But Cruella will just be asleep, like all humans," said Pongo.

"You forget. Cruella's *not* human."

"We were never *sure* of that," said Pongo. But it was true that they had once believed that Cruella might be some kind of devil. Perhaps the mysterious sleeping wouldn't affect devils! Still, he told Missis firmly, "Anyway, only dogs are awake. And she's certainly not a dog."

Before long they were in Camden Town, not far from Regent's Park where Pongo and Missis had once lived; then they hurried across Marylebone Road and along Langham Place past Broadcasting House.

Missis said, "There won't be any broadcasting as there are no humans awake. How Cadpig will miss television!"

Regent Street was very full and not only of swooshing dogs. There were also a great many dogs merely looking in the shop windows. And now there was more noise.

Dogs were chattering quite gaily. Missis heard one say, "Madam Cadpig's quite right. If we've come to London we might as well enjoy ourselves." No doubt Cadpig was trying to keep everyone happy.

Piccadilly was even fuller than Regent Street, but Pongo's army managed to get through and then went along Haymarket into Trafalgar Square. "Nearly there, now," said Pongo as they swooshed into Whitehall.

Then he wondered if he had spoken too soon, for the crowd was almost solid—and at the entrance to Downing Street it appeared to be *quite* solid. What was he to do? Cadpig had told him to let her know when they arrived, but there was so much noise that no bark would be heard.

"Well, we must do our very best thought waves," he said to Missis. And then he asked all the dogs in the army to help. "Just think, with all your strength, 'Cadpig, we're here in Whitehall'."

It worked magnificently. Within a couple of minutes a squad of Police Dogs were forcing their way through to Pongo. The leader said loudly, "All dogs of Madam Cadpig's own breed are to proceed to Downing Street. All other dogs are to proceed to Horse Guards' Parade."

Pongo felt responsible for the dogs who had joined him. He said, "Will they be well looked after on Horse Guards' Parade?"

The leader of the Police Dogs said, "They don't need looking after. Today no dog wants to eat, drink or even sleep. All they need is a place to sit. And there's no more sitting room in Downing Street. On your way, boys!"

Half the Police Dogs cleared a way to Horse Guards' Parade. And then the leader said, "Make way for the Dalmatians!"

Dogs fell back without resentment. Indeed, they were all wagging their tails and there were cries of "Long live Madam Cadpig and all her Dalmatian relations."

Missis said, "I hope I'm not looking smug, Pongo. I hadn't realized how important our daughter has become."

And so the Dalmatian army entered Downing Street.

5. The Cabinet Meeting

Cadpig was standing at the open door of No. 10. As a pup she had been unusually small and she was still on the small side for a full-grown Dalmatian. But, apart from that, she was an almost perfect specimen of the breed, with beautiful spots, wonderful dark eyes and a most fetching expression. Pongo and Missis had sometimes feared she might have become too grand for them, so they were touched to see how lovingly she greeted them, and all her family, giving a specially warm welcome to her devoted brother, Patch. She then spoke most graciously to all the other Dalmatians, remembering many names though it was around a year since she had left Hell Hall.

"Pretty manners," thought Missis proudly. "No wonder she's getting on so well."

Behind Cadpig stood a number of dogs whom she introduced as "My Cabinet." These were the dogs who lived with the members of the human Cabinet and were deputizing for them. "This is the Chancellor of the Exchequer," said Cadpig presenting a black Labrador. "He's longing to meet you, Father, because you're so good at figures."

"It's Mr. Dearly, not me, who's good at figures," said Pongo. "I can't do much more than put two and two together. They *usually* make four."

"With us, they've only been making three," said the Labrador. "But things may be better after the Chancellor's had this long restful sleep."

Cadpig was now presenting the Foreign Secretary, a plump, jovial Boxer. He reminded Missis of someone but she couldn't think who it was.

"And this dear friend is the Minister of Transport," said Cadpig, smiling at a prettily clipped brown Poodle. "It was she who got the traffic lights to work. Wasn't that brilliant?"

"I just thought about them," said the Poodle, "and, bless me, they happened!"

Other Cabinet Ministers were presented, also some dogs who lived with members of the Opposition. "That's the party that didn't win the last Election," Cadpig explained to her mother. "But of course we're all on the same side now."

"Everyone should be on the same side always," said Missis. "Think how much time it would save."

"But I've heard there's a catch in it," said Cadpig. "You

47

see, sometimes everyone gets on the *wrong* side." She then said she wanted a little talk with her parents before the Cabinet Meeting which would shortly start. "So will the rest of you go out into the garden? The Minister of Transport will act as hostess for me, won't you, Babs dear?"

The brown poodle said indeed she would and she and all the members of the Dog Cabinet escorted all the Dalmatians except Pongo and Missis, who tried not to look as important as they felt.

As the hall became emptier Missis gave a gasp. She was now able to see that, lying on the black-and-white marble floor, was a policeman. Of course he was asleep but, even so, Missis felt scared. She asked why he was there.

Cadpig said, "There's always a policeman here, to guard the house, and two policemen outside. The outside ones have been moved by the Police Dogs but I thought this one might as well stay where he is."

"I can't feel that policemen should be allowed indoors," said Missis. "Anyway, he makes the hall look untidy."

Cadpig said she would get him moved later, if she could think of any place to put him. "This house is so full of sleepers—secretaries and the like. Now I want you to see the Prime Minister."

She led the way to the lift, which obligingly opened its doors. Neither Pongo nor Missis had ever been in a lift and Pongo felt sure Missis would be nervous. He said quickly, "Couldn't we use the stairs?"

"Oh, the lift's perfectly safe," said Cadpig. "I know which buttons to press. Though today I'm working it by my thoughts."

"You mean, metaphysically," said Missis.

Cadpig looked impressed. "How clever of you to understand that!"

"Your mother has always been very metaphysical," said
Pongo.

The lift took them upstairs; then opened its doors to let them
out. Missis thanked it politely.

"This is the flat where we all live," said Cadpig, "but there's
no one at home but the Prime Minister. His wife's away. Quite
a good sort of woman but fussy about dogs getting on beds.
This way."

She took them into a bedroom. A Police Dog, lying by the
bed, stood up.

Cadpig said, "Here are my father and mother, come to help
us, Sergeant."

"And I'm sure they'll be able to, madam," said the Police Dog. "There isn't a Police Dog in England who doesn't know how Pongo and Missis rescued the stolen puppies."

Cadpig was looking anxiously toward the bed. "Any change, Sergeant?"

"None at all, madam—except that he seems to me to be smiling slightly."

"You're right," said Cadpig. "Oh, *good!* That must mean that he's really relaxing." She turned to Pongo and Missis. "How do you think he's looking?"

"Very peaceful," said Missis. "And younger than on television."

"He's an excellent color," said Pongo.

"Not too flushed?" Cadpig asked anxiously.

"No, no. Just healthily rosy."

"He's lost quite a lot of his chubbiness," said Cadpig. "That's because he's had so many worries. Well, this is one crisis *he* doesn't have to face."

Missis said, "I like him better than I expected to. I think that's because he isn't talking. He talks too much, on television."

"I agree," said Pongo. "He should just sit there with you on his knee, Cadpig, smiling kindly but saying nothing. Could you give him the hint?"

Cadpig shook her head sadly. "Clever though he is, he can't understand a word I say."

"That's our trouble at Scotland Yard," said the Police Dog. "We dogs learn so quickly, but none of us has ever managed to train a policeman."

Cadpig gave the Prime Minister a gentle pat and invited her

parents to pat him too, which they respectfully did. Then Cadpig said they must go down to the Cabinet Meeting. "Much as I hate to leave him."

"I'll guard him well, madam," said the Police Dog, standing to attention.

On the way to the lift, Cadpig said, "I want you to take the chair at the Cabinet Meeting, Father."

"No, no," said Pongo. "I shouldn't know what to say."

"Well, I don't either," said Cadpig. "And I'm terribly worried—and I mustn't, I mustn't let anyone but you two know. I'll tell you when we're in the lift."

The lift doors opened and they all got in. But when the lift had gone down only a little way, it stopped.

"Don't worry," said Cadpig. "I *asked* it to stop. This is the only place I can feel sure I shan't be overheard. There are dogs all over the house this morning. Oh, dear!" She suddenly drooped, looking helpless and pitiful, and gave a little moan.

"Now stop being silly, dear," said Missis briskly, "and tell us what's wrong."

Pongo said, "Has something happened that we don't know about?"

"No, it hasn't," said Cadpig. "And *that's* what's wrong. *Nothing's* happened and I can't find out what's *going* to happen. This morning everything was exciting—learning to swoosh, finding I could send my thoughts everywhere and tell dogs what to do. But now I wish I hadn't told them. Thousands and thousands have come to London and I don't know what to do with them."

"Well, send them home again," said Missis.

"But if I do that, they'll lose faith in me. And then they

won't want to see me on television when things are normal again. And that will be bad for the Prime Minister as well as me."

Pongo saw that his gifted daughter had bitten off more than she could chew—not a thing that often happens to a dog. He said firmly, "The dogs might as well be here as anywhere else, provided you avoid panic. You must let them know the situation's under control."

"How can the situation be under control when I don't know what the situation is?"

"I'll admit that's a bit tricky," said Pongo. "But about this Cabinet Meeting—"

"*Please* take the chair, Father!"

"Can't you and your father *both* have chairs?" said Missis.

"Of course there will be chairs for everyone, Mother. Taking the chair means being in charge."

"And that's what you must be, Cadpig," said Pongo. "You must represent the Prime Minister. But you may call on me to speak."

"What will you say, Pongo?" asked Missis.

"Ah!" said Pongo, in a meaningful tone.

"I don't think 'Ah' will be enough," said Missis.

"I meant that it will come to me, when it needs to. And it will come to you, Cadpig."

"No, it won't," said Cadpig miserably. "I've lost confidence."

"Then you must get it back at once," said Missis, who did not fancy being between floors in a lift with a Cadpig who had lost confidence. "And you can start by making this lift work."

"Perhaps I can't now," said Cadpig.

"Well, *I* can," said Pongo. "Today we can *all* open doors

and make lifts work." He directed a polite but powerful thought to the lift and it instantly moved downwards.

"Oh, Father, you're splendid," said Cadpig. "Though I *think* it would have moved for me."

The lift stopped suddenly. Missis felt frightened. Then the lift moved downwards again.

"That was just me, testing myself," said Cadpig. "Oh, thank you, Father. My confidence is coming back again."

The lift reached the hall and opened its doors. Missis, having hurried out, remembered to thank them. She thought it wise to keep on their right side—though, as far as Missis was concerned, their best side was the outside.

Cadpig led the way to the back of the house and into a large room which she said was the Cabinet Room. Up till today Missis had thought that a cabinet was a piece of furniture in which ornaments were shut away from puppies. But she had by now gathered that—in Downing Street—a Cabinet was a group of dogs who would help Cadpig to govern England, and this was the room in which they met. She need not have worried about a shortage of chairs. There were more than she could count, placed around a very long table. Tall windows opened onto a terrace which had steps leading down to the garden, where the Dalmatian army was being entertained by Cabinet Ministers. From the terrace, to which Cadpig took them, Missis could see over a wall to Horse Guards' Parade, which was packed with dogs.

Pongo said, "What a magnificent sight! It looks as if every breed of dog is represented."

"Except Corgis," said Cadpig. "They're all sitting outside Buckingham Palace."

The Boxer who had reminded Missis of someone came

bounding up the steps of the terrace. He said, "Is it all right by you, Cadpig, if I make one of your brothers my Private Secretary? He's a splendid fellow."

"Good idea," said Cadpig. "All Cabinet Ministers had better have Private Secretaries. I'll have Patch for mine. Hi, Patch, where are you?"

Patch came eagerly up the steps—only to be bowled over by the Foreign Secretary, who was swooshing down.

"Sorry, old chap," said the Boxer, helping Patch up.

"I haven't quite got the hang of this swooshing. The Minister of Transport says swooshers rank as vehicles and keep to the left, but I don't feel like a vehicle. Not hurt, are you? Good. Now where's my new Secretary?"

"Of course he'll have chosen Lucky," said Missis, proudly thinking how intelligent Lucky was. "Oh, good gracious! Look!"

The Boxer had joined Roly Poly, who was happily wagging his tail.

Pongo said, "Cadpig, dear, I'm not sure your Foreign Secretary has made a wise choice."

Cadpig laughed. "Oh, George is always putting his paw in his mouth. But he's a dear and so is Roly Poly, so they'll keep each other happy. And perhaps it's safer for them to get into trouble together rather than separately."

Missis said, "Bless me, I've just realized who the Foreign Secretary reminds me of. It's Roly Poly—though you wouldn't think a Boxer could look like a Dalmatian, would you?"

"It's something in the expression of their nice round eyes," said Cadpig. "I think the Minister of Transport had better have both Lucky and his wife as her Secretaries. She'll need a lot of help, what with the traffic and her topknot. Just arrange for that, will you, Patch? And then come back to me."

Patch, looking happy and capable, ran back to the garden and found Babs the Poodle, who gave her thanks to Cadpig.

"A pretty creature, isn't she?" said Missis. "Though I do think that topknot's a bit much."

"She's been known to have it tied up with a very fancy ribbon," said Cadpig.

A powerfully-voiced clock began to chime the hour.

"That's Big Ben," said Pongo. "How close we are to it here."

Missis carefully counted the strokes and was glad she only had to go as far as three, a nice, easy number.

Cadpig barked down to the garden. "Time for the Cabinet Meeting."

Members of the Cabinet, who had been chatting to the Dalmatians, came up the steps to the terrace. Patch came back to Cadpig and Lucky and his wife, Gay, followed Babs the Poodle. Missis expected to see Roly Poly come with George, the Foreign Secretary, but there was no sign of either of them. Missis looked around the garden and saw that they were standing by a door in the wall. The door opened (no doubt it had been asked to) and out they both went.

Missis said to Cadpig, "I fancy the Foreign Secretary will be late."

"Well, we can't wait for him," said Cadpig, taking her parents back into the Cabinet Room. "Now will every dog take a chair—but not the one with arms. That's the Prime Minister's and I shall represent him. Please sit on my right, Father. And Mother shall be on my left."

But Missis said she did not want to sit at the table as she

didn't know anything about politics. "When they happen on television I close my eyes and somehow manage to go deaf—unless *you're* appearing, Cadpig. Let me sit by the window here."

She wanted to watch for Roly Poly. What was he up to? She didn't agree with Cadpig that he and the Foreign Secretary might be safer together than on their own. Together, they might get into twice as much mischief.

"Well, sit where you like, Mother dear," said Cadpig, climbing up into the Prime Minister's chair. "Now attention, everyone!"

There was no doubt that Cadpig's confidence had come back. Missis was glad about this and proud of the impressive way her daughter outlined the situation. But it seemed to Missis that all the dogs already knew what the situation was and wanted to know *why* it was and what was going to happen next. Of course Cadpig had nothing to say about this and soon she was calling on Pongo to speak. She introduced him as "My famous father."

Missis remembered a speech Pongo had made to her on that cold night when he and she were setting out to rescue their puppies. It had helped her and she wished he would say something like it now.

Really, it was strange the way thoughts were dashing about today! It seemed that Pongo must know what was in her mind.

"Lady dogs and gentlemen dogs," he began. "Long ago when my dear wife and I were setting out on a perilous journey, I told her that dogs who are very well treated sometimes lose their liking for adventure and grow old before their time. Now I feel sure that all the dogs at this table are well treated, and though I don't say any of you are fat, you are quite well

covered. But I won't believe you are stodgy. I think you are all ready for anything. Am I right?"

All the dogs said "Yes, indeed" or "Hear, hear" and some of them banged the table with their paws.

Pongo then went on, "The question is, what are we ready *for*? But if we knew that, wouldn't the adventure be more *ordinary*? Isn't it more exciting not to know what lies ahead? Let us live excitingly from minute to minute and let us count our blessings. Think how much we have learnt since we woke up this morning. We can swoosh, open doors, bark by thought waves. And none of us is hungry, thirsty, too hot or too cold. Perhaps most important of all, we are completely friendly. Close to us here, on Horse Guards' Parade, there are hundreds—no, thousands—of dogs crowded together. But I have not heard one dog-fight. Have there been any?"

A vast number of dogs barked "No!" and Missis realized that Pongo was sending his thoughts out far beyond the Cabinet Meeting. Perhaps he was sending them all over England—she thought he must be because, from now on, whenever there were cheers they came to her like a great rushing wind. She could not have said if she was hearing with her ears or with her mind. She just *knew* the cheers were happening. And she felt prouder and prouder of Pongo. He went on saying encouraging things and telling all dogs how well they were behaving (so clever of him, thought Missis—how pleased she always was when the Dearlys said "*Good* dog!")

Finally he said, "My dear pet, Mr. Dearly, sometimes reads aloud to Mrs. Dearly, and my wife and I sit and listen. I remember once hearing of a famous Prime Minister who lived in this house who was always telling people to 'Wait and See.' That is what I say to you, oh dogs of England. Don't worry about what's going to happen. Wait and see!"

This provoked enormous enthusiasm. Missis happened to remember that Mr. Dearly had thought it a very annoying thing to say and many people hadn't liked it. Well, perhaps much depended on how it was said. Pongo said it magnificently and Missis thought it sounded splendid. Like all the other dogs, near and far, she barked delightedly and thumped her tail.

Cadpig sprang up in her chair and said, "Dogs everywhere! My father has told us what to do. Wait and See! Wait and See!"

WAIT AND SEE! WAIT AND SEE! The rushing wind of thought grew louder and louder. Missis began to wonder if it was healthy for thought to be so noisy and she was relieved when Pongo barked, "But let us wait and see *quietly*," and the cheering died down.

This came as a relief to Pongo too. He was thankful that he could now hear himself think. But he was also worried. How *obedient* the dogs were—and they were obedient to him! What a responsibility! Still, it could hardly be wrong to tell them to wait and see, as there was absolutely nothing else they could do.

At that moment the glass door to the terrace burst open and in came Roly Poly and George, soaking wet. They shook themselves violently, splashing all the dogs near them. One of these was Babs the Poodle, who protested loudly.

Cadpig spoke severely to the Boxer. "George, keep still! You should have got your shaking over out of doors. And you've missed the Cabinet Meeting. Where have you been?"

The Boxer said, "I was showing Roly Poly the lake in St. James's Park and he happened to say he could swim and I said I couldn't. He said all dogs can if they try and he'd show me how. So he did and now I can swim like anything."

"You both ought to be dried," said Missis. Oh dear, this was a job one needed humans for. Well, rolling on the carpet would help. She soon had George and Roly Poly rolling energetically. They got drier and drier and the carpet got wetter and wetter.

"That's no way to behave at a Cabinet Meeting," said Cadpig. "The Prime Minister never lets anyone roll. George, do get back to your office and see if any news has come in." She explained to Pongo. "It's the Foreign Secretary's job to deal with foreign countries."

"Did you get through to America?" Pongo asked.

"Not yet. But we got through to some dogs in Ireland who had managed to, and there seems no doubt that this mysterious sleeping is world-wide. We've talked to lots of European countries. George, do stop rolling."

"Right you are, Cadpig," said the Boxer. "Come on, Roly Poly, old man. We'll go and have a chat with the Continong."

But as George and Roly Poly galumphed to the door it was flung open by a Police Dog.

"Pongo and Missis!" he said dramatically. "You are urgently needed. A Sheepdog is calling you from the country. He says he has astounding news."

6. News from the Country

"Follow me!" cried Cadpig, dashing out of the room and to the lift, which instantly flung open its doors and took them up so fast that Missis hadn't time to feel nervous.

They got out at the top floor and Cadpig led them to a room where the window was wide open. Standing with their feet on the window sill were two Fox Terriers listening intently.

Cadpig joined them at the window and barked down to the

crowd of dogs in Downing Street. "Absolute quiet, please. Important news is coming through."

Instantly there was silence.

One of the Fox Terriers said to Cadpig, "This is a Very Important Sheepdog, madam. He's a General."

"Tell him Pongo and Missis are here," said Cadpig.

The Fox Terriers barked piercingly; then, as before, listened intently. After only a few seconds one of them said, "There he is!"

Cadpig beckoned Pongo and Missis to the window. They put their paws on the sill and leaned out as far as they could. At once they heard the General's rumbling bark. They answered him.

"Pongo and Missis?" said the General. "Yes, I recognize your voices. Amazing, this new invention. I got through to London at once. Well, now, prepare for a shock. The cats are awake."

"All cats?" said Pongo. There were millions of cats in England, weren't there? And many of them unfriendly to dogs. He foresaw clashes.

"No, no, not all cats. Just Mrs. Willow and your white Persian. They're both with me. And so is someone else who's awake. Young Tommy."

"Tommy?" gasped Pongo. "Then the emergency's over. All the humans will be waking."

"Oh, no, they won't," said the General. "All the other humans at the farm are still fast asleep and so are your humans at Hell Hall. I've just been up there, and Prince and I did our very best to wake them—actually shook them; well, it was in a good cause. They didn't stir and neither did the white cat's husband. She was upset about that until I explained to her."

63

"Please explain to me, too," said Pongo.

"It came to me in a flash. Well, actually, it came to Mrs. Willow first but I wasn't far behind. Do you remember, soon after you settled in Hell Hall, we made Mrs. Willow and the white cat honorary dogs? And Tommy—he and I could still talk each other's languages then, a kind of Dog-Human— asked if he could be one, too. So he and Mrs. Willow and the white cat are, well, sort of half-dogs."

"Let me have a word with the white cat," said Missis, who was longing for news from Hell Hall.

"Can't be done," said the Sheepdog. "As they're only half- dogs they can't do everything we do. They can't talk by thought waves and they can't swoosh. But they're fully awake and I'm thankful to say that they don't need food or drink. And it's a great comfort to have them, especially as Tommy's partly got back his knack of being able to talk to me. And he's full of bright ideas and so are the cats. And we simply must join you in London."

Pongo said "But how—if Tommy and the cats can't swoosh? The cats might ride on your back but Tommy couldn't."

"We've worked out a plan. Tommy will drive the Tractor. He's never *quite* driven it but he's sat with his father and been allowed to put his hand on the steering wheel. And he knows how to turn the engine on. Anyway, we've been practising and it seems that if my Jack Russell and I perch near him, with both the cats, and we all think hard about the Tractor moving forward, well, it does."

"How fast?" asked Pongo.

"Very, very slowly. In fact, it would take quite a week to reach London. But Mrs. Willow has worked out a scheme.

Wonderful brain she has—for a cat. I won't give you the details now, as you'll soon be seeing for yourself. But I'll tell you, that Tractor's never moved so fast in its life. We're starting at once."

"Well, good luck to you," said Pongo, wondering what on earth the tabby cat's scheme could be. "We'll be waiting for you in Downing Street."

"The white cat insists that we go first to that house where you used to live in Regent's Park. And she wants you to meet us there."

"But why, General?" asked Pongo.

"Can't tell you now but the white cat says it's *necessary*."

Then the Jack Russell Terrier was heard barking shrilly. "We ought to be starting, General. Let's get some action."

"That'll be enough from you," said the General ferociously. "But the cheeky pup's quite right, Pongo. Now you meet us at that house in a couple of hours. Signing off now."

The barking stopped. Cadpig, who had heard everything, said, "Well, it's best to humor the dear old gentleman. And you can take a look at the Zoo as you'll be so near."

"I'd forgotten about the Zoo," said Pongo. "Is all well there?"

"It was when I had my last report. All animals asleep except dogs—there are quite a few dogs attached to the Zoo. They're patrolling regularly. Dear me, I wonder if there are any *half*-dogs there? Wolves, for instance."

"I hope not," said Missis. She had seen wolves on television and didn't fancy them.

Cadpig said, "I suppose it's just possible that the General *will* get here in a couple of hours—today, anything's possible. So you might as well get off to the Zoo now, Father. Need

65

Mother come with you? I have to entertain some provincial ladydogs in the drawing room and I thought she might help me."

"The General asked for me," said Missis, who very much wanted to see their old home. And there was another reason why she wanted to go to Regent's Park, a worrying reason. She thought she knew why the white cat wished them to meet her there. But she wasn't going to tell Pongo, not until she had talked to the cat.

Cadpig said she could manage on her own and perhaps some of her brothers and sisters would like to see the house where they were born. "We'll go down and collect them. But I'll keep Patch to help me, if he doesn't mind."

"Patch would rather help you than see any house in the world," said Pongo.

They went down to the Cabinet Room and Babs the Poodle said she would willingly spare Lucky and his wife; Gay wanted to see her husband's birthplace. So in the end Pongo and Missis were able to take all their family except Cadpig, Patch and Roly Poly. Cadpig barked to the Foreign Secretary's office, hoping to reach Roly, but the Police Dog on duty there said the Foreign Secretary had taken him out to see London.

"They'll be all right, Mother," said Cadpig. "George is quite a dog-about-town."

Missis was far from sure that made things any safer.

Police Dogs escorted Pongo and Missis and their family until they were through the worst crowds and could swoosh to the Zoo without difficulty.

Missis didn't fancy the Zoo at all, but when she found that all the wild animals were not only asleep but also safely behind bars, she felt less nervous. The dogs attached to the Zoo were most polite and only sorry that Cadpig hadn't come. A keeper's dog said, "We were hoping to catch a glimpse of her. It's such a pity she can't appear on television as she does when things are normal."

Pongo wondered why she couldn't. Today, when dogs had such extraordinary powers, why couldn't they make television work? Surely it was just the kind of thing that they could work metaphysically. Indeed television seemed to him quite a bit metaphysical even when things were normal. He must talk to Cadpig about it.

All the Dalmatians were quite used to seeing wild animals, on television, but to see so many sleeping animals was very strange indeed. Elephants, lions, tigers, giraffes, monkeys, polar bears, seals and many, many others lay there utterly still, except for their gentle breathing. Missis need not have worried about the wolves; they slept as deeply as every other animal. Half-dogs they might be but they were not *honorary* half-dogs. Perhaps that made all the difference.

Birds in the aviary slept on their perches. And strangest of all were the sleeping fish in the aquarium. They might have been painted fish in painted water.

Long before they had seen everything there was to see, Missis said she thought it was time to leave. She could not really enjoy herself because of her secret thoughts. And she wanted to be at the Regent's Park house when the General and his party arrived, so that no time was wasted before she shared her suspicions with the white cat.

So they said goodbye to the courteous keeper-dogs, who were getting very busy as many sight-seeing dogs were now

coming into the Zoo, through the turnstiles which, today, worked without being pushed. And then Pongo and Missis led their family out and along the Outer Circle.

They had not gone far when they heard many dogs barking, and it was a special kind of barking which they recognized as cheering. What could it mean?

The cheering was coming from behind them. Pongo thought a halt, so that he could look back, and a moment later he saw the most astonishing sight. Coming across the bridge over the Regent's Canal, at a tremendous pace, was the Tractor.

At the wheel sat young Tommy, and near him were the General, the Jack Russell Terrier, the white cat and the tabby cat, Mrs. Willow. All of them were gazing straight ahead and none of them noticed the little group of Dalmatians—who saw, as the Tractor swept past, that it was being pushed by a dozen of the Dalmatians who had been left behind at Hell Hall. They were swooshing and so was the Tractor. Its wheels weren't touching the ground.

"It's become a Hover-tractor," said Missis. "How very metaphysical."

"We must follow it," said Pongo. "Quick swoosh."

They caught up with it just as it stopped in front of the house that had once been the Dearlys'. The Sheepdog, the Jack Russell and the cats got down, but Tommy stayed at the wheel and seemed to be talking to the Tractor.

"He's thanking it," the General told Pongo. "It's behaved magnificently. You'd think it was human."

"You mean canine," said Pongo. "Well, between you and it you've been marvellously quick."

"Prince lent me a dozen strong swooshers," said the Gen-

eral. "And we at the front helped by thinking forward thoughts, which is quite hard work."

Tommy now got down from the Tractor. Pongo and Missis greeted him affectionately and tried to understand what he said. Usually they did understand him, just as they understood most humans, but he was now talking half-Dog and half-Human, as he had when he was very young, and they couldn't get the hang of it.

"Needs practice," said the Sheepdog. "I can follow most of it now and he half understands me, which is more than any other human ever did."

The Dalmatians who had come with the Tractor had joined the ones who had been born in the Regent's Park house and Lucky was pointing out the kitchen window. He said, "Shall we go inside, Father? I expect the door will open for us if we ask it to."

Missis at once said, "The people who live here now might not like us to go in."

"But they'll all be asleep, Mother," said Lucky, who wanted to show his wife the broom cupboard where he had been born. He ran up the steps, willed the door to open and pushed it. But nothing happened.

"That's because we don't *need* to go in," said Missis. "And anyway, I don't want to see our home now it isn't ours."

Lucky's wife, who was looking down through the railings, said, "I can see the kitchen quite nicely, Lucky, and I can *imagine* the broom cupboard, if you describe it."

As Lucky had only slept in the broom cupboard for the first two weeks of his life he couldn't really remember it, but Pongo helped him out and described the whole house. All the dogs listened—that is, all except Missis. She drew the two cats aside and asked why they'd specially wanted to come here. She said she couldn't believe they'd particularly wanted to see the house.

"Well, I've nothing against seeing it," said the white cat. "In fact, I've very friendly feelings toward it as it was the first house I ever lived in where I was treated decently. But the house I really want to see is farther along the Outer Circle. And we must go inside. It's the house where I lived such miserable years with Cruella de Vil. I feel it in my bones that she's back in England."

"She is!" cried Missis. "Oh, I guessed you'd suspect her, and so do I. I'm sure she's causing this mysterious sleeping."

"Then she must be stopped," said the tabby cat. "I don't like the world without humans."

"We must get into her house and, well, *frighten* her," said the white cat. And she meant much more than she said.

Missis had always thought it wrong for any dog or cat to hurt a human, but she was highly in favor of *frightening* Cruella, so she said at once, "We must convince Pongo." Then she stared in astonishment.

Swooshing toward them at a tremendous speed and barking loudly was a Staffordshire Terrier. He pulled up when he reached them but, even so, knocked several dogs down.

"Sorry mates," he said. "Nobody hurt, I hope? (Nobody was.) Well, my old friends Pongo and Missis. Hope you haven't forgotten me."

"As if we could!" said Pongo. "You and your miraculous removal van once saved all our lives."

"Are *your* humans asleep?" said Missis.

"I'll say they are," said the Staffordshire. "And not for the want of waking. I was pretty rough with them before I found out that they couldn't help it, poor chaps. Not that I hurt them—I hope."

"So do I," said Pongo, knowing just how rough the Staffordshire could be. He lived with two removal men who called him names like "Canine Cannon Ball" and "Self-launched Bomb," but they loved him dearly.

"Just dropped in to see a pal at the Zoo," said the Staffordshire, "and I heard you were here. Well, perhaps you can tell me what's up with the world today. Think it's got anything to do with that old enemy of yours, the one who stole your pups?"

"*I* do," said the white cat. "And we ought to attack her."

The Staffordshire looked at her in surprise. "Didn't know there were any cats awake today."

"Both these ladies are honorary dogs," said Pongo. "And good friends of ours."

"Then they're friends of mine, too," said the Staffordshire, giving up the idea of chasing both cats up a tree—only in fun, of course, but cats never understood, they'd no sense of humor. But the white cat was talking sound sense so he said to her, "Well, if you want to attack the puppy-stealer, count on me. I told Pongo long ago that we ought to do her in."

"No, no," said Pongo. "This strangeness today has nothing to do with Cruella. Let's leave her alone." But he found everyone was against him.

The General said, "The woman's a thoroughly bad lot, Pongo. Remember, I saw more of her than you did, in the days when she owned Hell Hall. And the least we can do is to investigate her. Besides, I promised Tommy he should see her."

Tommy was already up on the Tractor, ready to start. The General, the Jack Russell and the two cats got up, too. Lucky said to Pongo quietly, "I think you'll have to let them have their heads, Father. But I'll help you to keep order. And all the Dalmatians will do exactly what *you* say."

But would the Sheepdog, Pongo wondered, and would the Staffordshire? They were both formidable dogs. And the cats were capable of dangerous clawing. As for the Jack Russell, he was barking fiercely, "Forward to kill Cruella de Vil!"

"Get into position, Tractor-pushers!" ordered the Sheepdog.

Pongo said he and Missis would lead the way. Their family and the Staffordshire helped to push the Tractor so it went at a tremendous pace.

"Faster, faster!" barked the Jack Russell.

"Pipe down, boy," said the General. "There's a legal speed limit in London. Better stick to it, Tommy."

"How?" said Tommy.

"Just think legal thoughts," said the General.

The Tractor slowed down a little but, even so, Pongo and Missis were rather afraid they might be run over. They were thankful when they reached Cruella's house. How well they remembered it and that snowy Christmas Eve when the white cat had invited them in to destroy Cruella's furs!

"Perhaps she doesn't live here now," said Pongo.

The white cat had sprung from the Tractor and run down the steps to look through the kitchen window. She called back to Pongo. "Oh, yes, she does. I can see the giant pepper-grinder she always used at meals."

Pongo now hoped they wouldn't be able to open the door. He told himself they wouldn't if they didn't need to.

But it seemed they did need to. The door of the kitchen swung open as if to invite them in.

So in they all went.

7. The Clothes that Clanked

The white cat looked around the kitchen and said, "Dirty, as ever."

Several dogs sneezed.

"That's the pepper in the air," said the white cat. "She must be using even more than when I lived with her."

Pongo was reading a recipe which lay on the table. It was headed "My Favourite Pie." He said, "Listen to this. 'Line a pie dish thickly with black pepper. Sprinkle with a very little meat. Put a thick layer of white pepper, then a thick layer of horse radish mixed with mustard. Top with red pepper. Serve very hot.' "

"You couldn't serve that cold, even if you froze it," said Missis.

Most of the dogs were sneezing now.

The Sheepdog said, "We'd better go upstairs. There may be less pepper there—though we may find worse things than pepper. Keep close to me, Tommy. You can't defend yourself as we dogs can."

Up in the hall, which was painted in violent colors forming angular shapes, Missis said, "These walls used to be green marble."

"Fake marble," said the white cat.

"And the drawing-room walls were red marble," said Pongo. "They reminded us of raw meat."

Missis peered through the open drawing-room door and said, "Now they're like the hall, only worse." As well as angular shapes there were angular faces with horrid expressions. And in the dim light that came through the drawn curtains some of the painted faces looked frighteningly real. Missis backed out hastily.

Pongo looked into the dining-room and warned Missis not to. "All the painted faces in there have very long noses. I think they're all portraits of Cruella."

"I suppose she *is* here?" said the General doubtfully. "The house seems deserted."

"She's probably upstairs," said the white cat, who had been practising her claws on a purple rug. "Let's go and see." She turned to the Staffordshire and asked him to come with her.

"It'll be a pleasure," said the Staffordshire, looking at the clawed rug. "I'd say you and I have the same idea, though you favor claws and I favor teeth."

Pongo said to the Dalmatians, "You are not to attack Cruella. She *can't* be to blame for what's happening today."

Missis said earnestly, "Oh, Pongo, you're wrong!"

Could he be wrong? Pongo began to fear he might be. There was something very strange about this silent house with its painted faces, something that felt menacing. And if Cruella *had* bewitched all the humans in the world perhaps they wouldn't wake up until . . . well, something was done about her. Anyway, he couldn't stop the white cat and the Staffordshire, who were already on their way upstairs. He hurried after them and so did all the others.

The white cat stopped outside a closed door and said, "That's where the de Vils slept."

The door slowly opened. Beyond it was complete blackness, from which came a mysterious rasping sound. The darkness and the rasping sound were so frightening that the white cat and the Staffordshire drew back, though both of them were brave animals.

The white cat said, "Often I can see in the dark but not in that kind of darkness. It's blacker than black."

Pongo, a born leader, said he would go in first.

"I'll come with you," said the Sheepdog.

"No, General," said Pongo. "You must stay with Tommy."

Missis came and stood shoulder to shoulder with Pongo. She was terrified but determined to act bravely, which is the bravest kind of bravery there is.

The Staffordshire said he was coming too.

"Then get on the other side of Missis," said Pongo, who knew it would be useless to tell Missis not to come. "And everyone else wait until I give the word to follow us. No, Lucky, you must stay with your wife. Bless me, who have we here?"

The Jack Russell had pushed his way forward, trembling with eagerness. Pongo admired his pluck but told him to take care of the General and Tommy. "And you two cats hold back. Remember you're only half-dogs."

The rasping noise had got louder and the room seemed blacker than ever. But slowly, slowly, Pongo, Missis and the Staffordshire moved forwards.

It seemed to Missis that the darkness was thick, as well as black. She felt that, if she opened her mouth, it would choke her.

"If only we could *see!*" thought Pongo.

Then the heavy curtains at the two tall windows parted and slowly drew back just far enough to let two shafts of afternoon light shine in. And what they shone on were two beds. In one bed lay Mr. de Vil, a small, worried-looking man. He was snoring loudly. That was the rasping sound which had been so frightening. It was certainly an odd sort of snoring, but now Pongo knew what it was it seemed to him more funny than frightening.

The Staffordshire said, "You wouldn't think such a little chap could snore so loud."

Cruella de Vil lay asleep in the other bed. There was nothing funny about *her*, though she did not, in sleep, look as frightening as when Pongo and Missis had seen her last, that Christmas Eve when she had chased them and all the puppies in her enormous black and white car. But she did not look pleasant and peaceful, as the sleeping Dearlys did. Her mouth was grim, her long nose seemed more pointed than ever, and she was frowning heavily. Perhaps she looked less frightening only because her eyes were closed, those black eyes with a streak of red in them. Even the memory of them made Missis shudder.

"First time I've seen a dame with black and white hair," said the Staffordshire.

Lucky called, "Can we come in now, Father?"

"Yes, if you keep quiet and don't crowd around the bed," said Pongo.

The white cat got there first and said, "Half her hair turned green with shock, after we destroyed her furs. I suppose she's had it dyed. No ermine sheets now, has she? That was the best night of my life, when I clawed them to bits."

"Funny kind of sheets she's got now," said the Staffordshire. "They look like tin."

"They'll be plastic," said the white cat. "When we drove Mr. de Vil out of business as a furrier he went in for making plastic raincoats. Perhaps there are some of them about." She flexed her claws hopefully and looked around the dimly lit room.

Some of the dogs were already exploring it and suddenly, mingling with Mr. de Vil's snores, there came a noise like metal hitting metal.

Missis cried, "Pongo, that factory we saw this morning! Clothes that Clank!"

Pongo then saw that there were racks of plastic coats, just as there had once been racks of furs. But it must be some new kind of plastic. No ordinary plastic raincoat could make the noise these coats made, as the curious dogs examined them. Clank! Clank! The noise got louder and louder. If

the de Vils had been wakeable, it would certainly have wakened them.

Young Tommy managed to lift a coat from the rack and held it in the light from a window. It seemed to be made of shining black tin. After a moment he dropped it, murmuring something.

"He says it's too heavy to hold," the Sheepdog explained. "The woman must be dressing herself in some kind of armour."

The white cat went to the fallen coat and put out a paw.

"Don't, dear," said the tabby. "You'd only hurt your claws."

"How right you are," said the white cat. "Nothing less than a tin-opener could damage that stuff."

Missis, who took an interest in clothes because Mrs. Dearly did, looked at the rack of coats—from a safe distance. Some of them were in bright colors, scarlet, emerald, sapphire, flame. Really quite pretty, Missis thought. She went closer, deciding they wouldn't hurt her if she didn't hurt them. At once she scratched her nose on a sharp edge. "Treacherous," she thought. "Well, what else could I expect from Cruella's clothes?"

But she no longer felt that Cruella herself was a menace. And even the white cat seemed to have given up any idea of attacking her old enemy. Only the Staffordshire looked as if he wanted to. He was staring fiercely at Cruella.

Pongo noticed this. He knew that the Staffordshire was a descendant of dogs who'd had to fight for their lives in the days when it was considered sporting to set dogs to fight each other, so he did not blame him for the savagery in his nature.

But this was no moment for savagery, so Pongo said firmly, "Don't touch her, my friend."

"You Dalmatians are softies," said the Staffordshire. "She was your enemy before and she may be again. And if we did her in while she's asleep, she'd never even notice it."

The Sheepdog said sternly, "You can't bite a sleeping woman. It would be like shooting a sitting pheasant."

The Staffordshire felt snubbed. Although he enjoyed his life, traveling around in the removal van, he had sometimes envied country-gentlemen dogs he had seen helping men with guns. He had thought he could get on well with such dogs. Now he knew they would spurn him. He hadn't had the faintest idea you mustn't shoot a sitting pheasant.

Then the General said tactfully, "Not that I don't admire your fighting spirit. You're a dog I'd have been glad to have with me that night I thought it *necessary* to bite the Baddun brothers who used to work for Cruella. And now, Pongo, we should leave this depressing house. My young friend, Cadpig, may have need of us."

Then the curtains at the windows drew together again as if they knew that light was no longer needed. Once the room was in darkness it became frightening again. Dogs hurrying to the door bumped into the racks of coats, which clanked more and more. Missis was thankful when everyone was safely out on the landing.

The white cat, looking back, said, "Perhaps we've been too soft-hearted. We'll never get another chance like that. Still, they say let sleeping devils lie, don't they?"

"They say let sleeping *dogs* lie," said the Sheepdog. "And they don't mean it. Every time I take a snooze someone wakes me up. It's usually young Tommy."

Tommy fully understood that this was a joke. He put his arm around the Sheepdog's neck and they led the way downstairs.

As the front door opened to let them out Missis said to Pongo, "It turned out that we didn't really need to get into Cruella's house. So why did the kitchen door open to let us in?"

"Because we needed to know that we didn't need to," said Pongo.

The front door slammed behind them all. Missis looked up at the bedroom window and thought about the black room filled with clanking and snoring, then thankfully took a deep breath of the warm afternoon air.

The Dalmatians who pushed the Tractor were getting into position.

"Pongo and Missis must now come *on* the Tractor," said the General. "We can't have the Prime Minister's parents down on all fours, while we're up there."

The Staffordshire was standing slightly apart from the other dogs. It would be lonely at home, but he feared he might not be grand enough to come to Downing Street. The General guessed this and said, "Please come on the Tractor. I'd be glad to have you on my staff during this time of danger."

"Sit by me," said the white cat.

"I'll be proud to, ma'am," said the Staffordshire. Never had he expected to like a cat so much.

Missis was so relieved at knowing she didn't have to be frightened of Cruella that she greatly enjoyed the drive back to Downing Street, through cheering crowds. The streets were as full as ever but the Tractor got through all right.

Dogs were still swooshing in from all over England.

"An impressive sight," said the General. "I suppose our clever little Cadpig knows what they're all swooshing here *for*?"

Well, not unless she'd found out since he last saw her, thought Pongo. But he didn't want to give his daughter away so he just said, "Ah!"

"Top secret, eh?" said the General.

"Oh, I think we shall all know very soon," said Missis. She was feeling *expectant*. It was a word she had learned before her puppies were born, when the Dearlys had often told people, "Missis is expectant." She had liked the word then and she liked it now. To her it meant being excited without being afraid. And how grand she was, sitting up here and being cheered like Royalty. She waved a graceful paw. Really, with their old enemy asleep, there was *nothing* to worry about.

Pongo was glad to see her relief but he didn't share it. He had never really believed that Cruella was now the enemy—

and he almost wished she were. For even if she was a devil, she was the devil he knew. As things were, he felt that someone, something, much more powerful than Cruella was in charge today. And that someone, something, was still *absolutely unknown*.

8. The Voice

olice dogs cleared a way into Downing Street and said they would take care of the Tractor. And a Police Dog in the hall said Cadpig was upstairs in the drawing-room. Pongo and Missis led the way. They found their daughter all alone, except for the faithful Patch, and looking very small in the large, beautiful room. She was also looking worried. But at once she smiled brightly and greeted the Sheepdog, the cats, and the Dalmatians who had pushed the Tractor.

"I must have a ride on the Tractor myself," she said. Then

she told Tommy how glad she was to see him, and when the Jack Russell was introduced she said she'd always wanted to meet one. And before anyone could introduce the Staffordshire she ran to him and said, "But you're our old friend, surely. You saved all our lives long ago."

"Wonderful memory," thought Missis.

"Wonderful pluck," thought Pongo, remembering how forlorn Cadpig had looked when they entered the room. He told her there was nothing to fear from Cruella.

"Good," said Cadpig and then asked if everyone would like to see the sleeping Prime Minister.

"We shan't be too many?" asked the General.

"No, no. I've been letting conducted tours go up all afternoon. I feel *he* would like it." She asked Patch to act as an escort, and then said to Pongo, "You and Mother won't want to go up again. Please stay with me."

As soon as the three of them were alone together, Cadpig's bright smile faded. She said she'd had a depressing afternoon, entertaining the provincial lady-dogs. "Good creatures, of course, but one grows tired of feminine chatter. Oh, dear! This is the time of day the Prime Minister and I used to watch the news on television together. He had a glass of sherry and I had a peppermint cream."

"I've always been fond of peppermint creams," said Missis.

"There's a box of them on the table, there—if you *could* fancy one, Mother."

Missis looked longingly at the box, but what she longed for was the longing for a peppermint cream, not the peppermint cream itself. She was so unhungry that she could not remember what being hungry felt like.

Pongo said, "At a time like this, one does feel the need for television. It somehow linked us all together. Do you think we could make it work?"

"But there can't be anything on, Father—with all the humans asleep."

Pongo's idea had been that Cadpig herself should be on television, to please her many admirers. But now he had another idea. He suddenly felt a *need* of television, that it could somehow help him. And today, dogs seemed to get what they *needed*. He looked toward the big television set. It wasn't quite like the one the Dearlys had and he didn't know which knob turned it on and, anyway, he couldn't turn knobs. Well he couldn't *usually*—but usually he couldn't turn door handles. Perhaps today . . .

He looked hard at the television set and thought about *need*.

Click! One of the knobs turned itself.

Only Pongo noticed this. He would say nothing yet, he would wait until—

A strange sound came from the television, a soft, musical wail, very high and sweet.

"Listen!" cried Missis, quickly looking at the screen, which gradually became luminous.

"How marvellous!" gasped Cadpig.

The three of them stared at the television, hoping for a picture, but the screen remained blank, just an oblong of pale light.

"You see? There's nothing on," said Cadpig sadly.

But at that moment the screen grew lighter, changing from a greyish white to a silver white, and then it grew so bright that it was as dazzling as powerful head lights of a car on a dark night. And as the screen brightened, the room darkened until the three dogs sat in utter blackness gazing at utter brilliance.

Then the edges of the screen darkened a little and the light seemed to be drawing all its radiance into the center where— brighter than ever and flashing even brighter—it assumed the shape of a star.

Missis cried, "Pongo! The dream I had last night! I saw a bright light that turned into a star—and it was this star. It was high above the stable roof."

"Do you mean you woke and saw it through the window?" said Pongo. "The stars were very bright last night."

"No, no. Mine was a *dream* star. It was much bigger and brighter than a real star. It was *this* star!"

"Yes, Missis, it was this star," said a voice from the screen.

It was like no voice the dogs had ever heard before. It was not the voice of a human or of any animal—and yet, strangely, it reminded Pongo of Mr. Dearly's voice, reminded Missis of Mrs. Dearly's voice and reminded Cadpig of the Prime Minister's voice. This made it comforting as well as awe-inspiring.

The Voice went on, "All dogs saw me in their dreams last night but few of them remember it as you do, Missis. But they *will* remember it. That is part of the plan."

"*What* plan?" said Cadpig sharply. "Tell me at once!" Then she added in her most winning tone, "*Please!* You see, I have so much responsibility."

"And you are managing very nicely," said the Voice, sounding amused. "With the help of your clever parents."

Missis said, "Goodness, I'm not clever."

"There are different ways of being clever," said the Voice. "You are intuitive—which means you can often understand things without reasoning them out."

"Would that be metaphysical?" asked Missis.

"Very metaphysical," said the Voice, still sounding amused.

89

"Now Pongo is more *brainy* than you are. Has it not been said that he has one of the keenest brains in Dogdom?"

Pongo was greatly flattered. Many dogs had thought him brainy in the days when he had been cleverer than Scotland Yard at finding his stolen puppies. But he hadn't done anything very dashing just lately. He said, "I'm afraid my brain has grown rusty."

"But the rust is wearing off fast," said the Voice. "It was clever of you to tell all the dogs to 'Wait and See.' That's kept them happy. And it was clever of you to turn the television on, even if I did put the idea into your mind."

"*You* did?" asked Pongo.

"I did indeed," said the Voice. "Oh, you and I can work together, brainy Pongo. And I can work with metaphysical Missis. As for Cadpig! Now how shall we describe Cadpig? Clever *and* intuitive. Very, very pretty. And, shall we say, just a trifle bossy?" The Voice was now quite playful.

"Well, don't I need to be?" said Cadpig. "With thousands of dogs waiting for me to tell them what to do?"

"And you shall tell them," said the Voice. "Now listen carefully. You must get my instructions through to every dog in England. Many of them can be reached by your thoughts but there are some dogs, often in lonely places, who have not yet learned to read thoughts. You must talk to them by the old-fashioned Twilight Barking. All dogs must be made to understand. At midnight tonight all dogs in London are to be in Trafalgar Square. All dogs in provincial towns are to be in town-hall squares or public parks. Country-town dogs are to be in market places. And dogs in villages and deep country are to be in open spaces, village greens or on tops of hills—places where they can see the sky. And all, all, are to be in their places by midnight."

"And then what will happen?" asked Cadpig.

"Oh, you must take your father's advice and 'Wait and See'," said the Voice.

And suddenly Missis felt frightened of it—or was it the word "midnight" that had frightened her? Only that morning she'd told Pongo she found midnight scaring—and now she was being asked to sit in Trafalgar Square at midnight waiting for something to happen. It would be very frightening indeed. But she kept her fears to herself, so she was so astonished at what the Voice said next.

"Yes, Missis, it *will* be frightening. But don't you sometimes enjoy being frightened? Don't you find it pleasantly exciting?"

"No," said Missis.

"*I* do," said Pongo.

"There speaks my brave Pongo," said the Voice. "And how does my little friend Cadpig feel about it? Is *she* frightened?"

"I haven't got time to be," said Cadpig. "What's worrying me is all the thought-sending and barking I'll need to do. Have I to send the news over *all* England? And how about Scotland?"

"Scotland, too, and Wales. You needn't reach across the sea."

"But isn't this thing happening all over the world?" asked Cadpig.

"Certainly it is. But you can leave the rest of the world to me, dear bossy Cadpig. Now each of you may ask one question. But that question mustn't be 'What's going to happen?'."

Instantly Pongo, Missis and Cadpig felt that was the one question they wanted to ask.

"Hurry up," said the Voice.

Pongo said, "Who are you?"

"Oh, that would be like telling you what's going to happen. Wait and see, Pongo. Wait and see."

Cadpig said, "If I need your help, how can I call you?"

"You can't. You must manage on your own. Now your question, Missis, and be quick. In five seconds I shall leave you."

Missis tried hard to think of some really important question but she couldn't, and already the star was less brilliant. At last she said, "What's happened to Roly Poly?" As far as she knew, he was still on the loose in London with George, the Foreign Secretary.

"Oh, that fat funny son of yours," said the Voice. "I'm afraid

I can't see him at the moment and I haven't time to look for him. I have to make appearances all over the world. See you at midnight."

The star vanished, leaving the screen empty. Then the television turned itself off, with a loud click, and the room, which had grown so dark, was lit by daylight again.

Cadpig said, "Did you like him?"

"Was it a him?" said Missis. "I thought it was a her."

"Oh, no, Missis," said Pongo. "But perhaps we'd better call it an it."

"Isn't that rather rude?" said Missis. "Suppose he, she or it can hear?"

"Well, a voice on its own is always called 'it'," said Pongo.

Cadpig said, "I hope it *can* hear. I want it to know that I liked it at first, but then I thought it was making fun of us—which wasn't a kind thing to do, when we're all so anxious." She looked hard at the television and added, "If you've anything to say about that, click on."

But nothing happened. And just then the party that had been up to see the Prime Minister came back. Pongo, Missis and Cadpig at once began to tell what had happened, and as the three of them barked at once it was very confusing, but at last they made themselves understood.

"Well, at least we know that there's someone in charge," said the General. "But who?"

Young Tommy, wildly excited, began talking his extraordinary language very fast. The General listened carefully and then said, "This may be important. Tommy thinks that whatever it was that talked to you must have come from Outer Space."

Pongo remembered the books of Science Fiction he had

seen in Tommy's room. The little boy might well be right. Pongo decided to ask him some questions. But that very instant the television turned itself on again, with a loud click.

This time there was no star. There was just the Voice, saying loudly, "Pongo, don't pry. Tommy, keep your silly ideas to yourself. Now, Cadpig, get busy or there will be dogs who don't know what they have to do at midnight and that will be *most unfortunate* for them." Then the television snapped off.

Tommy was looking hurt. The Sheepdog licked him affectionately and they had a few words together. Then the Sheepdog explained. "Tommy says it's all right. The Voice isn't as cross as it sounds. Tommy says his father has no patience with Science Fiction and is often very snubbing about it. But he's really the kindest of men."

"What's Tommy's father got to do with it?" asked Cadpig.

"Tommy says the Voice sounded like his father's."

"I must start work," said Cadpig. "It'll take me hours to get my thoughts over the whole country. And the Voice said there must be the old-fashioned Twilight Barking, too. Father, could you and Mother cope with that for me?"

"Willingly," said Pongo. "But not from Downing Street. We'll bark from Primrose Hill, as we used to."

"Splendid," said Cadpig, then she sent Patch for a Police Dog and gave instructions. "Clear a way for Pongo and Missis from Downing Street to Primrose Hill. All traffic lights are to remain green until they have passed."

When this had been arranged, Pongo and Missis swooshed downstairs, out into Downing Street and then along Whitehall. (All dogs made way for them and there were many barks of

"Bravo, Pongo! Wait and See!") Soon they reached Trafalgar Square.

Pongo said, "This is where we shall be at midnight."

"Dogs should be in their baskets at midnight," said Missis. "Oh, Pongo, I wish it was last night! Don't you?"

Pongo found he didn't. He said, "Think of it this way, Missis. We've had many, many peaceful nights in our baskets. It'll be fun to have just one midnight in Trafalgar Square."

"If it *is* fun," said Missis. She had felt so happy driving back to Downing Street on the Tractor, but not since she had heard that Voice. Then she reminded herself it had sounded quite kind . . . at first, anyway.

The last few minutes of their swoosh were across Regent's Park. That afternoon Missis hadn't had much chance to look at it. Now she liked remembering how often she and Pongo and the Dearlys had walked here when they were young married couples.

They crossed the Outer Circle and swooshed to the top of Primrose Hill. Pongo said, "How different everything is now, from when we barked to get news of our puppies. Then it was bitterly cold—you wore your beautiful blue coat. And the trees in the park were bare."

"It's hard to remember them bare," said Missis, looking down at the leafy tree-tops.

By now it was early twilight. The air was still soft and warm and there still wasn't a breath of wind.

"We must start barking," said Pongo. "*Real* barking, this time."

It was quite a while since they had joined in the Twilight Barking. Except in emergencies, as when the puppies had been stolen, it was only a gossip chain, a way in which dogs could talk to their friends. There was so much gossip always going on inside the walls of Hell Hall that the dogs there seldom barked to the outside world. If the General wanted a word with the Dalmatians he usually strolled along to see them. So Pongo and Missis were out of practice and a little worried in case their barking did not carry.

And at first they had reason to worry, for when they gave the three sharp barks which signalled that an important message was coming, no dog answered.

"We must bark louder," said Pongo.

So they tried again. They barked to the north, they barked to the south, they barked to the east and west. Still no dog answered.

"We simply mustn't fail Cadpig," said Pongo. "She's depending on us. Once again, Missis. And this time we'll make a special effort to the north. There was a splendid Great Dane over toward Hampstead who used to be a great help."

Again they tried—never in her life had Missis barked so loud. Still there was no answer. But they went on and on. And at last, floating through the summer twilight, came a great, booming bark.

"He's still there," cried Pongo. "He's still there and he's heard us!"

"Can I believe my ears?" boomed the Great Dane. "Is it really my old friends Pongo and Missis, after all this time, and on this most extraordinary day when the barking-chain has been at its worst. All these new-fangled thought waves have been so confusing."

Pongo said anxiously, "But you have had the thought waves, sir? You know what's been happening?"

"Well, yes. But thought waves are so vague. And there are

97

no set times for standing by to receive messages. Much as I admire your daughter, I wish she wouldn't toss her thoughts into the air just when the mood strikes her. And I can't make head nor tail of what she's sending out from Downing Street this evening. Why are dogs to go to Trafalgar Square? Why doesn't Cadpig say?"

"Because she doesn't know," said Pongo, and then told the Great Dane about the Voice, and how it had said that Twilight Barking must be used for dogs who couldn't receive thought waves.

"Well, that's sensible, at least," said the Great Dane. "And you'd better leave the whole job to me. I've had firm promises from friends north, south, east and west, to be standing by for Twilight Barking, thought waves or no thought waves. Now let's get it clear. Cadpig said dogs in large towns are to go to town-hall squares or public parks. Country-town dogs go to market places. Dogs in villages and deep country go to open spaces, village greens or tops of hills. Everyone to be there by midnight. Right?"

"Exactly right," said Pongo. "And you, yourself, will join us in Trafalgar Square?"

"Oh, I couldn't come all that way. I'm no longer a chicken."

"But it's easy if you swoosh, sir. Have you got the knack?"

The Great Dane said he's swooshed around the lawn a bit, but a dog of his weight felt a fool floating on air, and he'd just step out on Hampstead Heath at midnight. "That's a perfectly good open space. Now clear the line, will you? I've got a big job to do if I'm to get the barking chain started in every direction."

"Good luck," barked Pongo; then signed off.

Missis said, "What did he mean when he said he was no longer a chicken? Was he ever a chicken?"

Pongo laughed. "It was just an expression, Missis. He meant he was no longer young."

"But when he was young he was a puppy, not a chicken."

"He was indeed, Missis, dear," said Pongo.

Then they heard the Great Dane barking again as he started work. How well Missis remembered that booming bark bringing the first news of their stolen puppies! She was thankful that all those pups were now fully grown, sensible dogs, capable of taking care of themselves—all but Roly Poly; he was more than fully grown but would never be sensible. Where *was* he? She felt anxious about him but didn't mention this to Pongo. There was no point in worrying him.

Pongo had his own worries and he didn't mention these to Missis. The truth was that when he looked up at the darkening sky, already dotted with pale stars, and thought about midnight in Trafalgar Square, he was anxious about *all* dogs. What was going to happen?

9. In Trafalgar Square

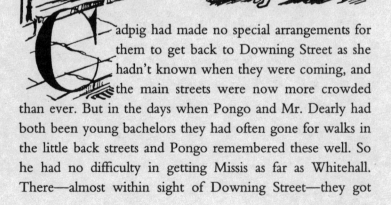

Cadpig had made no special arrangements for them to get back to Downing Street as she hadn't known when they were coming, and the main streets were now more crowded than ever. But in the days when Pongo and Mr. Dearly had both been young bachelors they had often gone for walks in the little back streets and Pongo remembered these well. So he had no difficulty in getting Missis as far as Whitehall. There—almost within sight of Downing Street—they got stuck, for masses of dogs were coming toward them, eager to reach Trafalgar Square.

Pongo sent thought waves to Cadpig but could get no answer, and there were no Police Dogs anywhere near to help. Then Missis said, "If we can swoosh just above the ground by believing we can, couldn't we rise higher and swoosh *over* the dogs who are coming toward us?"

"Well, we can *try*," said Pongo doubtfully.

"Then both together, and we must believe extra hard."

They rose up in the air like a couple of helicopters. Pongo stopped when he was well above the heads of even the tallest dogs, but Missis believed so hard that she rose up quite twenty feet.

"That's too high," called Pongo. "Come down lower."

"Oh, I like it up here," said Missis.

"But it's not safe. If you suddenly stop believing, you'll have so far to fall."

"Let's meet each other half way," said Missis.

So she came down and Pongo rose up, and they swooshed along about ten feet from the ground, waving to the dogs below and creating a great sensation.

"It was clever of you to invent this High Swoosh," said Pongo.

"Just metaphysical," said Missis.

They turned into Downing Street and came down neatly on the doorstep of No. 10.

The Police Dog on duty told them that Cadpig was holding a Cabinet Meeting, but when they got to the Cabinet Room they found that the meeting was over.

"None of us could think of anything to say," said Cadpig, "so we just passed a vote of confidence in ourselves."

There was no news of Roly Poly or George, the Foreign Secretary.

Cadpig was glad to hear that the Great Dane had taken over the Barking. "He'll do a splendid job. And I think I've made a good one of sending out thought waves. Dogs are quicker and quicker at picking them up and they're getting the knack of relaying them. What's worrying me now is how we're all going to get to Trafalgar Square. I've got Police Dogs there keeping room for us on the steps and terrace of the National Gallery, but they're finding it harder and harder to control the dog traffic in the streets."

Missis then explained her discovery of the High Swoosh and many of the Cabinet Ministers went out to the garden to practice it.

"Tommy and the cats won't be able to high-swoosh," said Cadpig. "They may have to be left behind."

"We'd better discuss it with the General," said Pongo.

They went up to the drawing-room, where the Sheepdog and his party were sitting, and explained the situation. Tommy and the cats were most unwilling to be left behind. They asked why they couldn't come on the Tractor.

"Because we can't possibly get the Tractor along Whitehall," said Cadpig. "It's packed solid with dogs."

"Why shouldn't the Tractor high-swoosh?" said Missis.

"I suppose it's just possible," said Pongo. "If enough dogs push it and think upward thoughts, as well as forward thoughts."

So they called all the Dalmatians in from the garden and went out into Downing Street to practise. There was plenty of room there now as all the waiting dogs had gone to Trafalgar

Square. And from the very first the Tractor showed willingness to rise up a good six feet.

"Then we'll start soon," said Cadpig, "and make sure of our seats." She sent Lucky and Patch to call all the dogs from the garden and get them into position, while she took a last look at the sleeping Prime Minister.

"Pongo and Missis must come on the Tractor," said the General, "and my young friend, Cadpig. It will increase her prestige."

Cadpig, when she came downstairs, was glad to agree. She had been so upset at leaving the Prime Minister that she hadn't enough spirit to manage a High Swoosh. Also, she felt that if she increased her prestige it would be good for the Prime Minister's prestige, too.

It was certainly a most remarkable procession that at last set out. Tommy was at the wheel of the Tractor, and the General, the Staffordshire, the Jack Russell and the cats sat near him. Cadpig and her parents sat on the Tractor's roof, so that the crowds could get a good view of them. All the other Dalmatians (except the missing Roly Poly) grouped themselves around the Tractor to help it with upward and forward thoughts. And behind, high-swooshing, came all the dogs who had been on duty at No. 10, now acting as an escort to all the Cabinet Ministers (except the missing Foreign Secretary). Babs, the Minister of Transport, high-swooshed most gracefully. Her top-knot was tied up with ribbon, which Lucky's wife had managed to put on for her.

The whole caninecade was wildly cheered as it passed over the heads of the dogs in Whitehall and Trafalgar Square. Police Dogs had managed to keep enough room for the Tractor to

come down, and soon all the dogs from Downing Street were settled outside the National Gallery.

Pongo, Missis and Cadpig sat high up between two pillars and could see right across the Square. It was solidly packed with dogs and so were all the streets leading to it. All dogs were well behaved but of course they were talking, so the noise was pretty deafening.

"It's hard to hear oneself think," said Missis.

"I don't want to hear myself think," said Cadpig. "I'm too nervous."

Missis, too, was nervous. It was night now and, though the stars were bright, they did not give enough light for her to be sure that those four huge lions in the middle of the Square were not live lions. She had caught a glimpse of them earlier and they hadn't been live then, but today anything was liable to happen. She felt almost sure she saw one of them move.

"I do wish the lights were on," she said.

"So do I," said Pongo, guessing Missis was nervous.

And then, as so often today, their wishes *worked*. The street lights lit themselves. Lights flashed on in the buildings around the Square and far beyond. Skyscrapers, dotted about London, turned themselves into hundreds of brilliant boxes, rising high above the small, old houses that clustered around them. There was enough light now for Missis to see that the lions weren't real, and what moved were the dogs sitting on the lions. She looked up to the top of the tall column in the center of the Square and saw a glow of light shining up on the figure of a man.

Pongo said, "Doesn't the statue of Nelson look fine?"

"Splendid," said Missis. "Pongo, who *was* Nelson?"

"He was the very great admiral who once said, 'England expects that every man will do his duty.' Only he didn't say it; he signalled it with flags."

"Very metaphysical," said Missis. "Quite like our thought-waving. Pongo, if you changed what Nelson said a little, it would be a fine thing to say to all the dogs here."

Pongo thought so, too. And when, soon, he was asked to make a speech, he finished up with "England expects that every *dog* will do his duty." This was an even bigger success than "Wait and See."

"No dogs seem at all anxious," said Cadpig, listening to the applause for Pongo's speech. "They're as cheerful as they have been all day."

"They're more than cheerful now," said Missis. "They're terrifically hopeful. Can't you feel it, Cadpig?"

Cadpig found that she could. Great waves of hopefulness seemed to be washing toward her. Hopefulness must be catching, she thought, suddenly feeling hopeful herself. In fact, she felt much more than hopeful; she felt happy. It was wonderful

to be Cadpig, the first dog Prime Minister, who had done such a splendid job all day. All Dogdom loved her and she loved all Dogdom. She felt *marvellous*.

And now Pongo, too, felt marvellous, as gay as when he had been a young bachelor dog courting Missis. As for Missis, she no longer felt anxious about anything. Of *course* Roly Poly would be all right; he always was. And how proud she was of Pongo and of Cadpig—and of herself. Had she not invented the High Swoosh? And here she was, in a position of honor, with her famous husband and her famous daughter.

Everywhere happiness was flowing freely. The General was telling the Staffordshire and the Jack Russell of that excellent night when it had been his duty to bite the Baddun brothers. All the Dalmatians from Hell Hall were wrinkling their noses

in enormous smiles. The Minister of Transport, Babs the Poodle, was doing a little dance with the Chancellor of the Exchequer, which was loudly applauded. All the Cabinet Ministers looked as if they had just won a General Election.

And the thousands and thousands of dogs in Trafalgar Square and the streets leading to it were now so happy that they were singing. They made a high, wailing sound which they all thought delightful. (Tommy and the cats weren't quite sure they liked it, and they weren't as deliriously happy as the dogs were; but they were perfectly cheerful.)

How beautiful the lights of London were! And Pongo now found that the brilliantly lit windows of the very tall buildings led his eyes upwards to the stars. Surely they were unusually large? They had been large last night, when he and Missis had

walked around the garden with the Dearlys (how long ago that
seemed), but they had not been *astonishing*, as these stars were.
They were not only large, they were also dazzlingly bright and
they seemed much closer than usual. And the more he looked
at them, the happier he felt.

He wanted to share that happiness so he barked very loudly,
"Look up, look up! Look up at the marvellous stars!"

All the dogs in Trafalgar Square and the streets leading to it
instantly did as he told them. Then the singing died away and
from every throat there came a sigh of happiness. It was like
the noise dogs make when they relax in comfort after a splendid walk, only it was much, much more happy. Then there
was absolute silence and stillness, with every dog gazing upwards as if spellbound.

Pongo had never known such happiness. It was like food to
the hungry, warmth to the shivering, love to the lonely. He

would have liked to ask Missis if she was as happy as he was but he could not; he could do nothing but look up at the stars. But soon he felt quite sure she did feel happy and all the other dogs did too—because, somehow, there was only happiness to feel.

He never knew how long the happiness lasted. Indeed, he soon barely knew who he was or where he was; it was almost as if he stopped being himself and became the happiness. But not quite. One little bit of his mind was still Pongo. And suddenly that little bit of his mind heard Big Ben striking. He counted the strokes—Boom, Boom, Boom. Was it midnight already? Was this the great moment? Would they soon know—what?

And then the lights of London went out, all together. But the stars were still there, as big and as bright and as close as ever. And one particular star looked even bigger and brighter and—yes, it was coming closer, much closer.

Missis gasped, "Oh, Pongo, it's going to fall on us!"

But the star did not fall—though what happened was almost more frightening. All the other stars went out, as the lights of London had gone out. Only the huge star remained, coming closer and closer. And then that, too, went out and there was no light at all, not so much as a glimmer. Everywhere there was inky blackness. And out of the blackness came the last boom of Big Ben, striking midnight.

Never in his brave life had Pongo been so frightened. Never before had he *trembled* with terror. He tried hard to be brave, tried to stop trembling. But he could not; he just shook and shook.

Then he found that Missis and Cadpig, between whom he was sitting, had moved closer to him as if for comfort, and they were trembling even more than he was. At once he told himself that he must not let them know he was afraid. They must feel that he was able to protect them, that he was a solid, rock-like dog. No solid, rock-like dog would tremble, so he just *had* to stop. There was nothing else he could do to help. He could not bark anything encouraging because no sound would come out of his mouth.

No sound would come out of any dog's mouth. Not one of the thousands of dogs who were assembled there could so much as whimper, let alone bark. Everywhere there was blackness, silence, terror.

Pretending to be brave helped Pongo to feel brave and gradually his keen brain began to work. Why was there no panic? The huge crowd of dogs might, at first, have been frozen with fear, but that would not last. Why did they go on being silent? There was not even any scuffling. Such absolute stillness was unnatural.

He suddenly knew that they were all being *controlled*, by someone, something, immensely powerful. And just as he realized this he saw a faint, hazy light high up in the air. The light grew strong enough for him to see that it was on the top of Nelson's column. For a moment the figure of Nelson could be seen and then Nelson vanished and there was nothing but the light, which soon became a dazzling blaze. At first it was a shapeless blaze but it gradually shaped itself into a star—like the one that had appeared on the Downing Street television but much, much larger and brighter. It was bright enough to illuminate all Trafalgar Square and the streets leading there. Indeed, Pongo thought it must be bright enough to illuminate all London.

For a few seconds the silence lasted. And then, from the heart of the star, a voice spoke. It was the same voice that had spoken from the television set, but now it was much more powerful and most wonderfully kind.

111

The Voice said, "Greetings to all dogs. Forget your fears. It was necessary for you to know darkness and terror, as a contrast to light and joy. But all that is over now. From now on there is nothing ahead of you but bliss."

A great sigh of relief came from all the assembled dogs.

The Voice went on, "That is, there will be bliss if you will accept bliss. The choice will be yours."

Missis whispered to Pongo, "What *is* bliss, exactly?"

"A special kind of happiness," Pongo whispered back.

It seemed that the Voice could hear whispers for it at once said, "Bliss is *perfect* happiness, Missis, which none of you have ever experienced—except for a little while tonight, before the darkness. Do you remember?"

"Oh, was *that* bliss?" said Missis. "Well, it certainly was marvellous."

"Yes, Missis, bliss is marvellous," said the Voice. "And I am offering it to you all for ever and ever."

Cadpig suddenly spoke up loudly and clearly. When first she had heard the Voice it had reminded her of the Prime Minister's and it still did. She was never afraid of the Prime Minister and she was always very firm with him. So now she said bravely, "May I ask, on behalf of all dogs, who you are?"

Many dogs barked, "Bravo, Cadpig!" And there were barks of, "Yes, yes! Please say who you are!"

For a moment there was silence.

"Goodness, I've offended it," Cadpig whispered to Pongo.

The Voice heard the whisper and said kindly, "No, Cadpig, I am not offended. You have the right to ask that question and it shall be answered."

Now the star blazed brighter and the Voice spoke louder, in a deep tone that was musical but also a bit like thunder— not frightening thunder, though; just gently powerful thunder, rolling around the midnight sky. The musical thunder said:

"I am Sirius, Lord of the Dog Star. For millions of years I have looked down on the Earth. I remember dogs when they were wild and savage animals. I have seen them change to tamed and often pampered creatures. And, wild or tame, I have always loved them and wished they could be with me on my lonely star. But never in the past did I feel I had the right to entice them away from the Earth. Now, at last, I have that right. For soon, through human foolishness, there may *be* no Earth—or no Earth as you know it now. And those few of you who survive will be desperate, starving wretches, fighting each other, eating each other, just in order to go on living a life that isn't worth living. Do you understand? I know one dog who does: your Prime Minister, Cadpig. She could not live at Downing Street without understanding. You know what I mean, don't you, Cadpig? Answer me."

Cadpig said, "You mean that humans may some day destroy the Earth with terrible bombs, in a terrible war. I know some humans believe that—but not all humans, and none of them want it to happen. And *I* don't believe it will. Why, the angriest dog in the world would not want to destroy all dogs— and itself—in order to win a fight. It wouldn't make sense."

"Well, it wouldn't make sense to a dog," said Sirius. "But dogs won't have any say in the matter. And neither will most humans. Oh, it may never happen. You're right in saying no one wants it to. But there *is* a risk, which gives me the right to rescue you all. Though perhaps I am only making it an excuse. The real truth is that I want you all so much."

The musical thunder of the Voice was now gently coaxing. It reminded Cadpig of the way the Prime Minister spoke on television when he specially wanted people to like him. At such times she always tried to help by putting her head on his knee and looking at him lovingly. Remembering this made her think of the poor dear man fast asleep in Downing Street and she said loudly. "But, Lord Sirius, how could we leave our pets?"

"Your *pets?*" The Voice no longer sounded gently coaxing. "You have no pets. You have owners. Oh, you pretend they are the pets. And some humans encourage you to pretend this and even say, 'Oh, my dog owns me.' But they know it isn't true and you know it, too. They put collars and leashes on you. They make you go where *they* wish. They shut doors, to keep you in or out as the fancy strikes them. Which of you, until today, has been able to open a door?"

Missis whispered to Pongo, "You can open doors that have

115

latches, not handles. You can even draw back bolts with your teeth."

Sirius said, "There's no point in whispering, Missis. I can even hear your thoughts. True, Pongo can open some doors, but there aren't many of those doors left. And anyway, he can't—nor can any of you—go just where you like, when humans are awake. Even Cadpig, who thinks she can always get her way with the Prime Minister, has never been able to get inside the House of Commons."

It was true. She had tried, and been carried home—oh, shame—by a policeman. Pongo guessed she was upset and put a steadying paw on hers.

Sirius went on, "Not that Cadpig isn't a most remarkable dog. And so is that great leader, Pongo, and so is metaphysical Missis who invented the High Swoosh; and that famous General, the Sheepdog, and his brave little friend the Jack Russell, and the gallant Staffordshire Terrier, and every member of Cadpig's Cabinet. In fact, *all* dogs are remarkable. Let us now praise famous dogs."

Sirius then mentioned every breed of dog. This took a long time as every breed responded with enthusiastic barks. And he did not forget dogs of mixed breed for whom, he said, he had a special admiration. "Such dogs are often both beautiful and intelligent. But what are they called by humans? They are called mongrels, a most insulting name."

One dog of mixed breed answered Sirius back. "Some of us are much loved. I have a good home."

"But your owners are always apologizing for you," said Sirius. "Haven't you heard them say, 'Oh, he's just a mutt. We call him Heinz or Fifty-seven Varieties.'?"

The dog didn't answer. It so happened that his name *was* Heinz. But what was wrong with that?

Sirius continued, "Anyway, there isn't one dog in the world even though he be the Champion of his breed, even the Best Dog in the Show—who isn't dragged about by his neck, bathed when he doesn't wish to be bathed, shut up, forced to obey. And many unfortunate dogs are beaten, starved, arrested by the police—"

"Oh, please, no!" murmured Missis.

"But it does happen," said Sirius. Then his tone became kinder. "Don't worry, Missis. It won't happen any more, to any dog—not if you join me on the Dog Star."

Cadpig said, "How could we? How could we ever get there? We should need millions of rockets."

Sirius laughed. "*Rockets*, Cadpig? Rockets are cumbersome, expensive and highly dangerous—though no doubt they are the best method of traveling into Space that men can think of. But the mind of a star can do better than the minds of men. Remember, we stars *live* in Space. Once you decide to come with me, I shall arrange it quite simply."

Missis said, "Should we just have to do an extra-High Swoosh?"

"Exactly, Missis. A very, very High Swoosh—quite easy if you wanted to."

"But suppose we stopped wanting to, half way?" said Missis.

"You won't be able to. You will be there in the twinkling of a star—once you *decide*."

Missis looked around Trafalgar Square. Perhaps some dogs would at once decide to go to the Dog Star. If so, would they instantly swoosh upwards?

117

Sirius knew what she was thinking. He explained, "It must be a mass decision, Missis—or rather, it must be a majority decision. Nothing will happen until all dogs have made up their minds. Then it will depend on what *most* dogs wish."

Like the General Election, thought Cadpig, which again reminded her of the Prime Minister. She would never decide to leave him. But suppose most dogs wished to leave the Earth, then she would have to. And then what would happen to him?

Sirius answered her thoughts. "He, and all other humans— and all sleeping animals—will simply wake to find a dogless world. And they won't remember there were ever such animals as dogs."

"But there will be our collars and leashes—and kennels and dogbeds and all sorts of things to remind them of us," said Cadpig.

"I shall work something out about that," said Sirius, "though it might be simpler to let them all go on sleeping for ever."

Cadpig had heard the Prime Minister say he would like to sleep for a week, but she was sure he would not like to sleep for ever. And what a dreadful thought—the world whirling around and around with everyone on it asleep—

Sirius interrupted her thoughts by saying gently, "Well, we'll let them wake up, then. And of course I know that many of you love humans. I admire your faithfulness and I *understand it*, because as well as being a star I am also a dog. See!"

Something very strange began happening at the top of Nelson's column. At the heart of the star a shape formed. At first Cadpig thought that Nelson was there again; then she saw that the shape wasn't a man. It was a dog, a white dog with black spots.

"Father! Mother! Look!" cried Cadpig.

Pongo and Missis, staring upwards, instantly realized: Sirius was a Dalmatian! But almost before they had taken this in, the General gasped gruffly, "Bless my soul, the fellow's a Sheep-dog!" Then there were delighted gasps from all the dogs sitting outside the National Gallery and then from all the dogs in and around Trafalgar Square, as each dog saw that a dog of its own particular breed was on the top of Nelson's column.

Cadpig said to Pongo. "What's the matter with them all? Surely there isn't any doubt that Sirius is a Dalmatian? I don't understand."

Pongo understood all right. Long ago he had heard Mr. Dearly say something about some saint who had been all things to all men. Well, Sirius was all things to all dogs—or, to be precise, he was all dogs to all dogs. Was that a good thing to be? Pongo supposed it must be, if it was something a saint had been. And it certainly proved how wonderful Sirius was.

The vision of dogs was fading now and the star was back in all its dazzling brilliance, and from it came the voice of Sirius sounding very gentle and very coaxing. "Well, now you have seen why I understand you all so well. And you can remember the bliss I gave you. Wouldn't you like to feel that bliss again?"

"Oh, yes, please!" barked many dogs.

"But some of you aren't sure," said Sirius.

Missis said, "I'm quite sure I'd like some more nice bliss, but not if it would mean coming with you. I couldn't bear to leave Mr. and Mrs. Dearly."

"Neither could I," said Pongo. But was he sure? He suddenly felt he wasn't sure of anything. He had begun to feel terribly confused and he didn't know why. But he did know this was no way for one of the keenest brains in Dogdom to behave.

The General, who up to now had not spoken directly to Sirius, said, "Look here, Sir, now that I've seen you, I feel I can speak dog to dog. And you, being the breed of dog you are, will understand my problem. I have obligations to sheep."

"The sheep will not miss you or need you," said Sirius. "And no humans will miss or need any dog. Dogs will simply be forgotten."

"What would happen to Tommy and our other two honorary dogs?" said the General.

"That depends on what they want," said Sirius. "Ask them."

Tommy and the cats had not been able to understand Sirius so the General had to explain.

Tommy instantly said, "I'll go with Sirius. I want to explore Space."

"Well, we don't," said both the cats, together. And then the tabby told the Sheepdog not to be fooled by such nonsensical ideas; and the white cat said some very rude things

about stars that didn't know their places and stay in them.

Possibly Sirius didn't fully understand cat language. Anyway, he merely said, "Then Tommy shall come and the cats shall stay. Well, that's something decided. And now may I hear from the rest of you?"

Thousands of dogs barked an answer. The noise was deafening—but no one could have said what the general wish was. Some dogs wanted to go with Sirius, some didn't. Many dogs wanted longer to decide and many, many dogs—in fact, most dogs—just said they didn't know. And then, one dog with a very loud bark said, "Let Pongo, Missis and Cadpig decide. We trust them. All day they have told us what to do. Let them tell us now."

And then it seemed that every dog for miles barked, "Yes, yes! Let Pongo, Missis and Cadpig decide!"

Pongo now knew why he was so confused. It was partly because of the noise and the excitement—he had always needed peace and quiet to think in. But most of all it was that he felt his mind was being invaded by the glorious, dazzling presence of Sirius. If only Sirius would let him think his own thoughts for a little while!

And Sirius miraculously understood. He said gently, "All right Pongo. Go into the National Gallery and think in peace. Take Missis and Cadpig with you, and any dogs you wish."

"How long may we have?" asked Pongo.

"One hour. It is now almost one o'clock. When Big Ben strikes two I shall expect your decision. Until then—so that you won't feel influenced by me—I shall leave you."

The star began to fade. A great sigh rose from thousands of dogs and Pongo knew what it meant. The dogs did not want to lose Sirius. And Pongo now found he didn't, either. He felt as he did when the Dearlys drove away from Hell Hall and didn't take him with them—only now he felt worse. Did that mean he loved Sirius—and loved him even more than he loved the Dearlys?

Now the star had completely vanished and Nelson was back on his column. The lights of London were shining again and so were the distant stars.

Cadpig said, "Which dogs shall we take into the National Gallery with us, Father? Shall the members of my Cabinet come?"

"Of course," said Pongo politely, though he did not think the members of Cadpig's Cabinet were particularly bright. "And all our friends who came from Downing Street with us must come too." Then he spoke to all the dogs in Trafalgar Square. "Please keep as quiet as you can so that we can hear ourselves think. But remember we're only trying to decide what's best for you all and if any dog feels he has something terribly important to say, we hope he will come in and say it."

A dog with a shrill voice barked. "I think I speak for many of us when I say we miss Sirius. We feel lonely."

"Yes, yes!" The words seemed to come from thousands of dogs.

"So do I," said Pongo.

Surely this loneliness meant that he and all the other dogs wanted to be with Sirius? But Pongo told himself he mustn't decide too quickly, mustn't mind the loneliness. Perhaps it was a trick Sirius was playing on them. He had said he was leaving them so that they would not feel influenced by him, but perhaps he knew how much they would miss him and that leaving them was his most powerful way of influencing them.

The doors of the National Gallery had silently opened.

Slowly Pongo, Missis and Cadpig led the way toward them. Big Ben began to strike one o'clock.

Perhaps, thought Pongo, the next hour would be their last on Earth. Perhaps, just in one short hour, all the dogs in the world would be on their way to a star.

11. What Answer?

Pongo had never been inside the National Gallery. Picture Galleries, he knew, did not admit dogs, which was something he had always regretted as he was fond of pictures. And now, alas, when he could have had the run of the place, it was no moment to look at them. He led his party across the dimly lit entrance hall, up the wide steps and into a long gallery. The light here was almost as dim as in the entrance hall, but across the gallery was an archway beyond which the light was brighter and—

Pongo couldn't believe his eyes. There was a horse there, with a rider on it, an upright horse fully awake, and so was the rider. Then the sleepers were waking up! Humans would soon be in charge again! Dogs need not have this tremendous responsibility of deciding their own fate.

Then he saw the horse and the rider were only painted, in a large picture. They were not real—and yet, somehow, they *were* real, in a way Pongo couldn't understand. He only knew that they made him remember men and horses very vividly and feel very fond of them.

He and all the dogs with him settled down on the polished floor of the gallery. Then Pongo took a vote. He found that only Tommy and the cats had made up their minds. Tommy still wanted to go with Sirius, the cats still wanted to stay on Earth. But after a moment Cadpig said, "I wish to stay. I can't *believe* the Prime Minister won't miss me."

This made a great impression on Cadpig's Cabinet, all the members of which now said that, if she stayed, they would.

Then Lucky said, "Father, I feel sure all the Dalmatians from Hell Hall will want to do what you and Mother decide to do."

All the Dalmatians from Hell Hall at once said, "Hear, hear!"

Missis said, "And of course *I* shall do what *you* wish, Pongo."

Pongo turned to the General who said he was an old dog to learn new tricks, but Sirius seemed a decent fellow and if Tommy wanted to go—"Not that I hold with people coming here from Space. I've always thought Space should keep itself to itself."

"I shall follow my General," said the Jack Russell.

"Thanks, lad," said the General, gruffly.

Pongo looked at the Staffordshire, who said, "I'm out of my depth, mate. Space sounds very airy-fairy to me, but I must say that bliss stuff was like a good kip by a warm fire after a slap-up meal. And naturally, I liked the look of Sirius."

Of course you did, thought Pongo—knowing that, to the Staffordshire, Sirius would have looked like a Staffordshire.

Cadpig said, "Father, there are far more Dalmatians from Hell Hall than there are dogs in my Cabinet. So it's what *you* decide that will count. Unless, of course, a majority of the dogs in the world disagree with you."

"It's no use thinking about that," said Pongo. "All we can do is to make our own choice. How much will you mind if I decide to go?"

"I don't know, Father. In a way, I *want* to go—if I can go with a clear conscience. I only know that *I* can't decide to leave the Prime Minister."

So that leaves it all to me, thought Pongo—and I just don't know what to do. He was puzzled that he should even consider going off with a star to a star. Even if the Dearlys did not miss him, would not he miss them, most terribly? Of course he would, and yet he still felt drawn to the star. What was this mysterious attraction? He had once heard Mrs. Dearly quoting a poem about "the desire of the dog for the star" (she had said "moth," not "dog," but that must have been a slip). Was it, then, natural for dogs to be drawn toward stars?

Oh, if only someone would explain to him and give him some really good advice! He looked toward the painted horse and wished it could be a real horse who would talk to him. Horses could be very helpful. He remembered the horse that had saved him and Missis and all the puppies they were rescuing, when gipsies had locked them in a field. But the painted

126

horse could do nothing, except look very noble—and somehow that was a little bit of help.

It was at that moment that he heard a dog barking "Pongo, where are you?" in the entrance hall, below. Surely he knew that booming bark? He barked back, "Here, sir—up the stairs!" and, a couple of seconds later, into the gallery at full tilt came the Great Dane from over toward Hampstead. And not only the Great Dane. Riding on his back was a tiny creature. A white kitten? No, more like a white puppy. But somehow it looked too grown up to be a puppy. Could it be a miniature dog?

"How splendid that you managed to get here, sir," said Pongo. And the Sheepdog—a General recognizing another General—rose, wagging his tail.

"Talk about swooshing!" said the Great Dane. "Part of the time I seemed to fly."

"That's the *High* Swoosh," said Missis. "*I* discovered it."

"Well, it took me by surprise and my little friend nearly fell off. By the way, don't mistake him for a puppy. He's full grown and three years old—a Chihuahua, ridiculous name for a breed, but he can't help that, can you, Sam? He's my very good friend, sleeps in my bed and acts as a hot-water bottle. Well, Pongo and Missis, we meet at last face to face. And I know who *you* are." He wagged his tail at the Sheepdog. "We've often sent messages to each other over the Twilight Barking, and we will again, when this Emergency comes to an end."

"But what end will it come to?" Pongo slipped in quickly.

"Do you mean you're in any doubt? Aren't you going to send this star back where it belongs?"

"We're not quite sure yet—"

The Great Dane cut Pongo short. "I knew it, I knew it! I said to Sam—he came out to Hampstead Heath with me—I said, 'They'll be fooled, all those dogs in Trafalgar Square.' Crowds are always fooled. They get so worked up that they can't think for themselves. I know about these things because I live with a Professor who often talks about them. All you dogs are the victims of mass hysteria."

Missis was shocked. Dogs as well as humans suffer from hysteria and she never felt it was safe even to mention the word. She said nervously to the Great Dane, "Surely that lovely bliss wasn't hysteria?"

"Now I'll tell you about bliss, Missis," said the Great Dane. "It was all part of a clever trick. First this Sirius fellow works us up into enjoying ourselves and then he plunges us into total darkness—I'll admit even I was scared when the stars went out—and then he appears and lights things up again. Well, naturally we feel relieved so we're pleased to see him. He'd worked up a marvellous entrance for himself."

"Bliss was more than just enjoying ourselves," said Pongo.

"Perhaps it was a bit more," said the Great Dane, grudgingly. "The fellow's certainly a very clever trickster."

"I didn't feel he was a trickster," said Pongo. "I felt that he loved us."

"Well, even Sam and I were fooled at first. But we soon found him out when he started changing himself into dogs. To me, he looked like a Great Dane and to Sam he looked like a Chihuahua. Now, apart from being ridiculous, that's dishonest. I take it that all you dogs saw him as being of your own breed?"

There were excited murmurs from all the dogs in the gallery.

"But I don't think he meant that to be dishonest," said Pongo. "It was to make us feel he understood us all."

"You know what humans feel about people who are two-faced," said the Great Dane.

"*I* don't," said Missis. "I didn't know there *were* any people with two faces."

Pongo explained hurriedly, "It just means—well, people who aren't sincere."

"Exactly," said the Great Dane. "And as there are getting on for one hundred breeds of dog, Sirius is one-hundred faced. And if you think that's a sincere thing to be, I don't."

Cadpig felt the Great Dane was being a bit bossy. So she said in rather a haughty voice, "If I might speak a word or two—"

"Who's this?" said the Great Dane, glowering.

"My daughter—at present our Prime Minister," said Pongo.

129

The Great Dane's manner became charming. "What, Cadpig? Honored to meet you, my dear. You're a very clever dog. Surely *you* don't want to go with Sirius?"

"As a matter of fact, I don't. But I think you're being unfair to him. He said he wanted to save us from The Bomb. Surely that's a real danger? I'm always hearing about it."

"So am I," said the Great Dane, "from my Professor. But Sirius can't possibly know that his star will be a safe refuge. My Professor says the next war's quite likely to be fought in Space—while we sit down here safely watching it on television. Now it's nearly two o'clock. Let's all get ready to say to this fellow, 'Sirius, go home.' Don't you *want* to, Pongo?"

Pongo had begun to feel he did. The loneliness he had felt when Sirius vanished had grown weaker and his loyalty to the Dearlys had grown stronger. (Surely he had never *quite* felt he could leave them?) He even felt a loyalty to the whole world that he had always known. But he couldn't believe that Sirius was a trickster. And he remembered that great sigh he had heard from thousands of dogs when Sirius disappeared. He said quietly, "But it isn't only what *I* want, sir. I have to decide on behalf of so many other dogs. And I'm nearly sure that most of them wish to join Sirius."

"Pongo," said Missis. "I think some dogs wish to speak to you."

Peering into the gallery were three dogs of mixed breed, one large, two small. All of them looked in poor condition and seemed very nervous. Pongo at once invited them in and, as they drew nearer, he saw that they were pitifully thin. This was particularly noticeable with the largest dog, because his bones were so big. He had a fine head and intelligent eyes; and though his dark coat was now matted, it was easy to see that he could be a handsome dog if well fed and well groomed. He came in a little ahead of the other two and was obviously the leader.

Pongo welcomed all three dogs and asked what they wished to say.

The big, bony dog said, "We speak for all the lost dogs. Some are from Lost Dogs' Homes. Some are strays. Some did not come to London because they could not believe they would have the strength. But those of us who are in Trafalgar Square, over a hundred of us, have talked to many dogs who could not be here—as you know, today our thoughts can travel anywhere. And they all feel as we do. You said that any dog who had anything important to say might come and say it. And to us, this is very, very important."

"Then of course you must tell me," said Pongo. He spoke in a kind, encouraging tone, but his heart sank. He had almost been convinced by the Great Dane that he must refuse to go with Sirius—but surely these pitiful creatures would want to? Surely they would wish to escape from their unhappy lives on Earth?

"Thank you," said the big, bony dog. "I should tell you first that we admire Sirius and believe in him. And we are deeply grateful for this wonderful day. Some of us had forgotten what it was like, not to be hungry. And today we have hardly felt like lost dogs—because, in a way, *all* dogs have been lost. I mean they have all been on their own with no humans to depend on. So we have not felt envious. Oh, none of us will ever forget this day that Sirius has given us!"

"And so you want to go with him?" said Pongo.

"*Oh, no!*" said the big dog. And the two smaller lost dogs also said "No!" in very shrill voices.

"But why not?" said Pongo, much astonished.

"We are not ready," said the big lost dog. "We want our lives here first. Always there is hope for us. Nearly all strays are taken to Lost Dogs' Homes—and then, very often, kind people come and offer them homes. Most of us can remember homes. Many of those homes weren't good ones and many of us were turned out, deliberately lost. But we had loved the people who treated us so unkindly and we want our chance to belong to someone again."

"You could belong to Sirius," said Pongo.

"That wouldn't count," said the big lost dog. "*Everyone* would belong to him. We all want someone of our very own."

The Great Dane said kindly, "And I hope you get someone.

132

You all deserve to. And now, Pongo, hasn't that helped you to make up your mind? It's time you did,"

It was, indeed. Big Ben had begun to strike two. And at that moment the room was flooded with light. Pongo knew where the light was coming from. Sirius, the blazing star, was back on top of Nelson's column. And as the great clock finished striking, they heard the musical thunder of his voice.

"I am here, Pongo!"

"Send him away, Pongo!" said the Great Dane.

"Tell him, not yet!" said the big lost dog.

Pongo, Missis and Cadpig led the way to the steps and down them to the entrance hall, with all the other dogs following. But even when Pongo went out through the doors into the dazzling light, he did not know what he was going to say. Oh, he knew he must refuse to go with Sirius, but how could he put it, how was he to sound both kind and strong? And when he came face to face with the blazing star he wondered if he had the strength to say it at all.

He did not have to. For Sirius, who could read the thoughts of all dogs, already knew. From the heart of the star came the great voice saying, "So the answer is 'No'. And it comes not only from you, all you dogs here in London. I can hear it from all over the world. And I know now that there could not be any other answer. Of all creatures, dogs have lived closest to mankind and they will never desert mankind. And though I do not think such devotion is deserved, I can admire it. And it is something in men's favor that they can inspire it and, in their way, return it. May you never regret your choice, oh Dogs of the World."

The Great Dane said, "Sir, I have misjudged you."

"But you were quite right to call me one-hundred-faced,"

said Sirius. "And when I am back in Space, in all my loneliness, I shall comfort myself by being every breed of dog there is. I shall *imagine* it. And imagination can be more real than reality, though that's something even I can't explain. And now we must be business-like." The deep musical voice became brisk. "All dogs must be home before sunrise, because then you will all be ordinary dogs, without power to swoosh or to open doors."

"Some of us live farther away than others," said Pongo.

"That will be allowed for. All dogs will reach home in time, provided they swoosh steadily and on no account turn back. Remember, the special powers given to you will only last just long enough to get you home. But there's no need to panic. All crowds must break up in an orderly way. Those on the outside must leave first. Pongo, you and your party must wait until Trafalgar Square is cleared."

"But will dogs know their way home in the dark?" asked Missis, anxiously.

"All they will have to do is to think forward thoughts toward their homes and swoosh steadily. Now I must leave you. I have a longer journey than any of you."

Pongo saw that the star, though still brilliant, was growing smaller. He called loudly, "Shall we ever see you again, Sirius?"

"You can always see me in the Dog Days of high summer, when I shine my brightest—if you remember to look."

"Oh, we will, we will," barked very many dogs. And then, as the star grew smaller and smaller, every dog in and around Trafalgar Square barked, "Goodbye, Sirius, goodbye!"

"Goodbye!" The voice that came from the dwindling star was now little more than a murmur. And then every dog heard a strange sound which was like a soft summer breeze stirring the leaves of many trees.

"What was that, Pongo?" asked Missis.

Pongo said, "Perhaps it was the sigh of a lonely star."

Now there was only a tiny point of light high on Nelson's column. And in another second even that had vanished. Trafalgar Square was in total darkness. Then the lights of London came back and quite ordinary stars were twinkling in the sky (if any stars are ordinary). And the Great Dane and the Sheepdog, speaking at the same moment, told Pongo it was time for action and all dogs must be hurried on their way.

"Then you two Generals do the hurrying, please," said Pongo, who was feeling very much upset. And so, he saw, were Missis and Cadpig who kept saying, "Oh, poor Sirius! Oh, poor lonely Sirius!" So Pongo comforted Missis, and Patch comforted Cadpig, and the two Generals very loudly told dogs how to get out of the Square. And by the time it was cleared Pongo was quite himself again—which he certainly needed to be, if he was to get his large party safely home. He hoped Sirius had made allowance for the extra swooshing power needed for the Tractor, with Tommy and the cats on it.

"We must go as fast as we can," said Missis. "It would be dreadful if Tommy didn't get home by sunrise."

"It would be dreadful if any of us didn't get home by sunrise," said Pongo. "But don't worry, Missis, dear. We shall."

But would they, *all*? Pongo earnestly hoped that Missis would not suddenly remember something which all the excitement had driven out of her mind—for if she did, he would never get her to leave London. *Roly Poly was not with them. Where, oh, where was Roly Poly?*

12. A Race with the Sun

Now that the Square was cleared, Cadpig was in a hurry to get back to Downing Street, as the Prime Minister often woke in the night and would be most upset if she wasn't there. She said a loving goodbye to all her family, especially to Patch, and promised to send messages by the Twilight Barking.

"I hope we shall soon see you on television," said Patch.

"Oh, I'm sure you will. And I heard the Prime Minister say that the next time he has to be out of England he'll send me to stay at Hell Hall, so we shall meet again very soon. How I wish you could all be with me when the Prime Minister wakes up!"

"*We* want to be with the Dearlys when they wake up," said Pongo.

"Ah, the dear, dear Dearlys," said Cadpig, but her thoughts were really with the dear, dear Prime Minister.

The dogs in Cadpig's Cabinet left with her, to return to their own homes. The Staffordshire left for St. John's Wood and the Great Dane, with Sam the Chihuahua on his back, set off for Hampstead, after arranging to keep in touch with the Sheepdog and the Jack Russell. (The Jack Russell had taken a great fancy to the Chihuahua because the tiny creature made him feel such a big, strong dog.) The three lost dogs had already gone, with all the other lost dogs, to the Battersea Lost Dogs' Home. All were taking this chance to get into it, knowing they would be fed and have the chance of being adopted by kind people.

Pongo assembled his party. Tommy, the cats, the Sheepdog and the Jack Russell mounted the Tractor, and the Dalmatians who had brought it to London got into position for the return journey.

"You and I will lead the way, Missis," said Pongo. He knew that if they lined up in rows of four—as they had, when coming from the country—she would instantly realize that Roly Poly wasn't beside her. Now, perhaps, she wouldn't notice it. Anyway he gave her no time to think. He told all the Dalmatians who weren't pushing the Tractor to fall in behind him and Missis, and then quickly barked the command, "Quick swoosh for Suffolk."

It was surprising how quickly the visiting dogs had got out of London. Already the streets were deserted except for a few dogs standing outside their own front doors.

"Very different from this morning," said Pongo. "Are you glad we're on our way home, Missis?"

"Yes, Pongo," said Missis. "But something's worrying me. And I can't think what it is."

"Don't try to," said Pongo. "Just keep your mind on swooshing steadily."

"Yes, Pongo," said Missis. But she still sounded worried.

Pongo said, "Missis, dear, if you should suddenly remember what's worrying you, don't let that stop you swooshing—or the dogs behind will stop, too, and the Tractor may bump into them. Now just let's think of getting home to our good beds and the Dearlys."

"Oh, *yes!*" said Missis happily, and she thought about this so hard that they had swooshed out to the suburbs before she began worrying again. If only she could find out what she was worrying about! She felt sure it must be important.

Pongo noticed that her pace was slackening. "Just a little faster, Missis, dear," he urged. "Think forward thoughts."

Forward thoughts! What did that remind Missis of? Who was it that, this morning, had thought a backward thought? It was Roly Poly! Where was he? *That* was what had been worrying her! Oh, how could she have forgotten?

She gave a quick cry and almost stopped swooshing but Pongo urged her on. "Steadily, steadily, Missis. Just keep up your pace. Now, what is it?"

She told him, finishing by saying, "We must go back."

"No, Missis," said Pongo firmly.

"But we can't leave Roly behind. Pongo, please stop swooshing. Let me talk to you."

Pongo saw that she couldn't go on, feeling as she did. And the whole army could do with a few minutes' rest. So he barked an order to slow down, making sure that the Tractor-pushers understood, and called a halt.

He then explained to Missis why he had felt they must start without Roly. "We'd no way of finding him. And I had to do what was best for us all—as I must now. At sunrise we shall lose our power to swoosh. We can't risk being stranded miles and miles from home."

"But the sun won't rise for hours yet," said Missis.

"It will. Summer nights are short. And remember, Sirius warned us we must on no account turn back. Roly will be all right, Missis. Sooner or later George the Boxer will bring him back to Downing Street and he'll be kindly treated."

"But no one will know where he belongs. He isn't wearing his collar—and Cadpig can't *tell* anyone he's her brother."

"Perhaps she can *hint* it," said Pongo.

Missis shook her head sadly. "We may never see him again. But it'd be something if I knew he was safe. Let's see if Cadpig has any news of him."

Missis at once began barking, calling Cadpig. But the only answers she got were from near-by dogs.

Pongo said, "I'm afraid we've lost our power to reach Cadpig by thought waves. And we *must* swoosh on."

Already the night sky was paler. Pongo felt anxious. What *counted* as sunrise? Would they be all right until they actually saw the sun or would they stop being able to swoosh as soon as darkness changed to gray dawn?

139

"Just one more bark, first!" begged Missis. "And please help me!"

"We'll *all* help," said Pongo, and gave the word, "Every dog is to bark with Missis, calling Cadpig. Three times! Now!"

The noise was tremendous. But after the third bark there was dead silence.

"We've done our best, Missis," said Pongo gently, and he warned everyone to be ready to start swooshing.

"Listen!" cried Missis.

Pongo listened, then said, "That's just a faint bark from some dog a mile or so away."

But Missis was now wildly excited. "That's not just *some* dog. That's Roly Poly!"

Again Pongo listened. The bark *was* like Roly's. Were they getting through to London?

"Roly, my darling!" barked Missis. "Where are you?"

And now there was no mistaking the answering bark. "I'm here, Mother—coming as fast as I can. Please wait for me!"

Then the tabby cat, on the Tractor, miaowed loudly, "I can see him!" And a moment later Roly Poly, swooshing at full tilt, was knocking dogs over right and left. He just managed to pull up as he reached his parents.

"Where *have* you been?" cried Missis.

But Pongo said, "You're not to tell us until we're safely home. Just get into line between your mother and me. Now all dogs at the ready! Quick swoosh!"

After a few minutes Missis whispered to Roly. "Are you tired, Roly? Are we swooshing too fast for you?"

"Oh, this is nothing after what I've done today," Roly whispered back.

"No whispering!" said Pongo sternly. "Save all your breath for swooshing." He was thankful that swooshing needed so little breath, but wanted to be on the safe side in case extra speed was needed.

Soon they were right out of London. They knew this first by the sweet fresh smell that came from the fields. Pongo looked anxiously at the sky. It was still, he told himself, a night sky but only just. He had seen it look like this when there was a moon behind clouds. Tonight there was no moon and he knew that, gradually but certainly, the dawn was coming. He called a halt and asked if every dog felt capable of swooshing faster. All including the Tractor-pushers, said they did.

"Splendid," said Pongo. "Missis and Roly, stop whispering. Now off we go." And he set a faster pace.

At this speed they simply streaked through the countryside. Soon they were in North Essex, soon through it and into Suffolk. But the dawn was keeping pace with them. By the time they were through Sudbury the sky was no longer a night sky.

"Faster!" Pongo commanded.

And now they went so fast that Pongo feared it might be too much for Missis. "Are you all right?" he asked her.

"Yes, Pongo," said Missis. "But it isn't my idea of a pleasant swoosh. This morning everything was so peaceful—and so still. Now the wind's awake. I'm just a little afraid my ears may blow off."

But they were still with her when at last the village nearest to Hell Hall was reached and a halt called, so that the Jack Russell could jump from the Tractor and run to his home. (All the other dogs from the village were already back.) Then it took only a minute to reach the farm.

"Get to bed quickly, Tommy," said the Sheepdog. "We must leave the Tractor in the road." (Tommy's father never could understand how it got there.) "There isn't a minute to spare. Look at the eastern sky, Pongo."

Pongo saw with dismay that there was a faint flush of pink. He was about to command, "Quick swoosh" when he realized that, though the tabby cat was safely home, the white cat wasn't and she couldn't swoosh. "You must ride on my back," he told her.

But the white cat refused—though politely. "I'm quite a weight, these days, with all the good food I get. I'll just walk home. And if the gates won't open for me, I can climb the wall—without any help from Sirius. So off you go."

"Then *quickest* swoosh," ordered Pongo.

The pink flush in the sky was growing stronger.

"Faster, faster," cried Pongo.

Now he could see the walls of Hell Hall, now he could see the gates, firmly closed. Would they open?

The Dalmatians halted outside them.

"Please, please, kind gates!" begged Missis.

The gates swung inwards—and there, waiting on the lawn, were Prince and Perdita and all the Dalmatians who had remained at Hell Hall.

"Oh, we were so afraid you wouldn't get here in time," said Perdita.

"Did *you* see Sirius, too?" asked Missis.

"I think all the dogs in the world saw him," said Prince. "And if I understand him rightly, we should all get to our beds instantly. At any moment the doors will close—and refuse to open for us."

Pongo nodded. "Every dog to his bed," he commanded.

The dogs who slept in the stables converted into kennels went as fast as they could—and Pongo noticed that they *ran*, now; they didn't swoosh. The magic was fading.

"Now upstairs, quickly," he told Missis.

"Do just let me hear where Roly's been," said Missis.

Roly Poly was one of the dogs who slept in the kitchen. He was on his way there now but he turned back.

"Oh, I just went to Paris," he said, trying to sound casual.

"You didn't, you couldn't have," said Missis. Surely Paris was in France, across the sea? "Oh, Pongo, I *must* hear about this!"

They were in the hall now. Pongo said to Prince. "You and Perdita run upstairs and *stop* the bedroom door from closing. And bark if it tries to. Now, Roly!"

Roly Poly said, "It was George. He's always wanted to go abroad. The Foreign Secretary—I mean the human one—is always going, but he can't take George because of the quarantine laws. So after I taught him to swim this morning, he thought we might both risk swooshing across the Channel—and we did it quite easily; we didn't even get our feet wet. And then we swooshed to Paris and it was wonderful. We had lots of fun. Then we were told to look at the sky at midnight, and we saw Sirius—on top of the Eiffel Tower. And he *noticed* us, he knew we were English dogs. And he said we could have a little extra swooshing power, to get us home in time. That's how I managed to catch up with you."

144

"Did you like Paris better than London?" asked Missis.

"You can talk about that tomorrow," said Pongo.

From upstairs Prince called, "This door is beginning to feel restive."

"Upstairs instantly!" Pongo told Missis, giving her a push.

She went obediently but called back to Roly. "Did you get on well with the French dogs?"

"Splendidly," said Roly. "And you should have seen George with the French lady-dogs. Ooh, la, la!"

Pongo and Missis hurried into the Dearlys' bedroom.

"Now you can let the door have its way," said Pongo.

The minute Prince and Perdita left the door, it very firmly closed. And all over Hell Hall doors could be heard closing, the kitchen door, the front door, the doors of all the kennels and—last of all—the tall iron gates clanged together.

"How well and peaceful the dear Dearlys look," said Missis, getting into her much-loved basket. "*Won't* they be surprised when they wake up and find out they've missed a whole day?"

"I don't think they *will* find out," said Pongo. "And I don't think they, or any humans, will ever know about this day we've lived through. And perhaps many dogs will forget it."

Missis said she never would, and Perdita, now settling in her basket, said she wouldn't either.

"But perhaps we shall think of it as a dream," said Prince, as he too settled down. "And in some ways it was like one, with so many things happening at once. Pongo, how was it that Sirius could talk to all the dogs in the world, in so many different places, all at the same time?"

Pongo shook his head. "I just don't know."

"Oh, *I* do," said Missis brightly. "In Space there probably aren't any clocks. And where there are no clocks there's no

145

such thing as time. But it's simpler to believe it was all done by magic. Magic's so easy to believe in."

"Yes, indeed," said Perdita.

"Though there's a new word for magic now. It's 'meta-physical'. I'll explain that to you, tomorrow, Perdita." Missis relaxed in her basket, then said in a surprised tone, "I'm *hungry*! How nice! Now I can look forward to breakfast. Of course I haven't minded going without food today—I haven't missed it. But I do believe I've missed missing it. And I'll tell you something else. I think there would be a catch about that nice bliss. After a while, you wouldn't notice it. Oh, hello!"

The white cat had climbed in through the window. She said, "It's like that night I climbed through your kitchen window in Regent's Park, after I ran away from Cruella de Vil."

"Oh, dear," said Missis. "How dreadful it is to think that Cruella will soon be waking up."

Pongo grinned. "Well, at least we shall always hear her coming, in those clanking clothes. Go to sleep, Missis dear."

The white cat joined her husband and gave him a fairly hard push. She adored him but that was no reason why he should have more than his fair share of their basket. He did not stir and soon she, too, was asleep. And so were Missis and Prince and Perdita—and, of course, the Dearlys. Only Pongo was still awake.

He remembered how, only yesterday morning, he had lain here hankering for adventure. Well, he'd had the adventure, and he was very, very glad it was over. He couldn't imagine ever longing for another. How fortunate he was! He looked lovingly at the sleeping Dearlys.

And suddenly he was frightened. Why hadn't they wakened? True, the dogs had talked in whispers, but early morning whispering usually woke the Dearlys who always said, "Quiet!," very firmly. Why were they so *heavily* asleep? Perhaps they *weren't* going to wake.

Then Pongo noticed a marvellous sound. Outside, birds were twittering, lots of birds. If the birds had woken up in the normal way, then so would the Dearlys. And then a shaft of early sunlight shone full on Mr. Dearly, who half opened his eyes, then turned over and slept again.

All was well, Pongo told himself, gazing at the rising sun. Mr. Dearly, when walking around the garden under the stars, had said that Sirius, the Dog Star, rose with the sun, though one couldn't see stars in the daylight. Was Sirius there now? And could he still read the minds of dogs? Just in case, Pongo sent him a message. "Perhaps one day, Sirius, we shall be ready to join you and accept bliss. But not yet. You see, we do have quite a lot of bliss already."

And then Pongo, feeling as young and happy as a puppy, rolled over on his back and went to sleep with his four paws in the air.